SOFT, SWEET AND GENTLE

She thought as the revolver was so light and yet so easy to use that she would certainly take it with her the next time they went on a long journey to the North or even, although her father might disapprove, to London.

As she took it out, she realised that it was loaded and there was also a box full of bullets, which she would surely need if she used it.

'I am certainly not going to leave this for Alister,' she said to herself.

As she picked up the revolver, she was thinking how carefully her father had taught her to handle it.

And how pleased she had been when he said – and it was the biggest compliment he could ever pay her – that she shot as well as any man.

She felt that her father would be hurt and upset at the idea of her having to leave The Castle, but there was no point in arguing with Alister, who had obviously made up his mind about her.

'I am just an exile from everything I love,' she told herself miserably.

Then suddenly to her surprise she heard a man's voice shouting,

"What the hell do you think you are doing?"

THE BARBARA CARTLAND
PINK COLLECTION

Titles in this series

SOFT, SWEET AND GENTLE

BARBARA CARTLAND

.com

Barbaracartland.com Ltd

THE BARBARA CARTLAND PINK COLLECTION

Dame Barbara Cartland is still regarded as the most prolific bestselling author in the history of the world.

In her lifetime she was frequently in the Guinness Book of Records for writing more books than any other living author.

Her most amazing literary feat was to double her output from 10 books a year to over 20 books a year when she was 77 to meet the huge demand.

She went on writing continuously at this rate for 20 years and wrote her very last book at the age of 97, thus completing an incredible 400 books between the ages of 77 and 97.

Her publishers finally could not keep up with this phenomenal output, so at her death in 2000 she left behind an amazing 160 unpublished manuscripts, something that no other author has ever achieved.

Barbara's son, Ian McCorquodale, together with his daughter Iona, felt that it was their sacred duty to publish all these titles for Barbara's millions of admirers all over the world who so love her wonderful romances.

So in 2004 they started publishing the 160 brand new Barbara Cartlands as *The Barbara Cartland Pink Collection*, as Barbara's favourite colour was always pink – and yet more pink!

The Barbara Cartland Pink Collection is published monthly exclusively by Barbaracartland.com and the books are numbered in sequence from 1 to 160.

Enjoy receiving a brand new Barbara Cartland book each month by taking out an annual subscription to the Pink Collection, or purchase the books individually.

The Pink Collection is available from the Barbara Cartland website www.barbaracartland.com via mail order and through all good bookshops.

In addition Ian and Iona are proud to announce that The Barbara Cartland Pink Collection is now available in ebook format as from Valentine's Day 2011.

For more information, please contact us at:

Barbaracartland.com Ltd.
Camfield Place
Hatfield
Hertfordshire AL9 6JE
United Kingdom

Telephone: +44 (0)1707 642629
Fax: +44 (0)1707 663041
Email: info@barbaracartland.com

THE LATE DAME BARBARA CARTLAND

Barbara Cartland who sadly died in May 2000 at the age of nearly 99 was the world's most famous romantic novelist who wrote 723 books in her lifetime with worldwide sales of over 1 billion copies and her books were translated into 36 different languages.

As well as romantic novels, she wrote historical biographies, 6 autobiographies, theatrical plays, books of advice on life, love, vitamins and cookery. She also found time to be a political speaker and television and radio personality.

She wrote her first book at the age of 21 and this was called *Jigsaw*. It became an immediate bestseller and sold 100,000 copies in hardback and was translated into 6 different languages. She wrote continuously throughout her life, writing bestsellers for an astonishing 76 years. Her books have always been immensely popular in the United States, where in 1976 her current books were at numbers 1 & 2 in the B. Dalton bestsellers list, a feat never achieved before or since by any author.

Barbara Cartland became a legend in her own lifetime and will be best remembered for her wonderful romantic novels, so loved by her millions of readers throughout the world.

Her books will always be treasured for their moral message, her pure and innocent heroines, her good looking and dashing heroes and above all her belief that the power of love is more important than anything else in everyone's life.

"Every man in my experience likes a woman to be soft, sweet and gentle – and he is far more likely to fall in love with a woman who is."

Barbara Cartland

CHAPTER ONE
1860

Lady Georgina Lang walked into the study and saw a pile of letters on her father's writing table that she knew she would have to answer.

She had just come from his funeral that had taken place very quietly in the village Church which was actually on the Earl's estate.

It was still hard to realise that her father, who had meant so much in her life, was dead.

She would never ride over the fields with him again or hear him giving her sharp orders that she must obey.

It seemed extraordinary that she was now alone in her home and she really had no idea what her future would be.

Her father had filled her life to such an extent that she could not imagine how she would manage without him.

The tenth Earl of Langfield had always been a law unto himself and he had never expected anyone to disobey his orders or in any way to contradict them.

He was a very good-looking man, tall and almost Regal in his attitude to life.

He had longed, as other men had done before him, for an heir to his title, his castle and his huge estate.

He had married, in the most perfect manner, the daughter of a Duke.

As he was so rich and important and she was very beautiful, it had seemed on the surface a perfect marriage, not only from the Social point of view, but because they might have been made for each other.

The Earl's title dated back to Cromwellian times, although early Langfields had distinguished themselves in battles both on land and sea.

One of the most prized possessions in Langfield Castle was the Family Tree. It had been kept up to date year by year since it was first started soon after William the Conqueror and his wife were crowned King and Queen of England.

The tenth Earl was undoubtedly in love with his beautiful wife, but at the same time he would not have married her if she had not been suitable to become the Countess of Langfield.

As they were described as one of the best looking couples in the Social world, it was clearly obvious that their children would be as handsome as their father and as beautiful as their mother.

Then, for some reason that the outside world could not understand and were far too polite to ask, there was no baby to be baptised in the Church where they had been married.

The Family Tree would seem to come to an end with their wedding.

Then, almost like a miracle, eight years after they had enriched the County by giving the best parties at The Castle, it was whispered that the Countess was with child.

It was a subject the whole neighbourhood talked about and speculated on.

"He's always wanted an heir," the men said to each other. "It seems extraordinary that he's waited so long."

"She had always looked an extremely healthy girl as well as being so beautiful," the women said. "I expected by this time they would have had at least three or four children."

No one, however, had ever been brave enough to ask the Earl why the nursery in The Castle was empty.

There was then a sigh of relief at the chance of it being filled.

Georgina was born a few days before Christmas.

She naturally had no idea when she came into the world that she was an overwhelming disappointment to her father.

The Earl had been certain that the child his wife was carrying would be a boy and he had gone through the family names to decide which of his ancestors had been the most distinguished and the most interesting.

There was little doubt that it was Admiral George Lang, who had demolished almost the entire fleet of the enemy he was fighting by his own brilliant leadership.

There had been books written on him at the time and he had been rewarded by the King who had given him the most brilliant decoration available.

"My son will be named George," the Earl had trumpeted. "He will also bear my name and that of my father."

He had it all planned out and decided that George would have the best Tutors available, then he would be sent to school at Eton and he would finish his education at Oxford where he himself had obtained a degree.

It seemed just incredible, after all the trouble he had taken, that the baby who came into the world just before the festivities of Christmas were to be doubled and trebled by his heir's arrival should be a girl.

What was more the Countess had a very difficult time and the doctors attending her made it very clear to the Earl that it would be impossible for her to have another child.

Because he was an intelligent man, he was able to hide his disappointment from the world outside, but those who knew him intimately were aware of how much he was upset by the information the doctors had given him.

He could not bear to think that, after all the love and care he had given to The Castle and the estate, no son of his would take his place.

There was, in fact, only a distant relative to inherit when he died.

He controlled himself as he had learnt to do since he had been a boy until the moment when his daughter was about to be Christened.

Because she was a girl the Christening was to take place in the Chapel that had been built in The Castle three centuries earlier.

No relatives were invited and the Countess was not well enough to leave her bedroom. The baby was therefore carried to the Chapel by her nurse.

It was actually when the local Vicar, who was also the Earl's private Chaplain, took the baby girl into his arms that something extraordinary happened.

Because he had been so upset that the much-wanted baby should be a girl, the Earl had not discussed with his wife, who was still very sick, or with anyone else, what her name should be.

He was still thinking of the child as George because of the Admiral's career, which had been uppermost in his mind during his wife's pregnancy.

Then, when the Vicar asked for the child's name, without considering his answer, the Earl replied,

"George!"

Thinking he must have misheard what the Earl had said, the Vicar proceeded to baptise the baby as 'Georgina' and the Earl found it impossible to say anything.

So Lady Georgina was baptised and the majority of the household and the Earl's relatives, when they heard of it, thought that it was a delightful name.

It was one that had not been used in the family before.

If the Earl had secretly hoped that he might have another chance of having an heir, he learnt that the only possibility would be if his wife died and he could marry again.

The doctors had told him that, while she could not possibly give him another child, she would live a normal life span if she was properly looked after and did not exert herself in any way.

As the Countess was still very young and beautiful, the doctors pointed out to the Earl that he was an extremely lucky man as his wife might easily have died, as a number of other women had done in similar circumstances.

Instead she should be with him for at least what was a usual lifetime.

If the Earl was upset by such a prediction, he was too much of a gentleman to show it.

He was charming and loving to his wife as he had always been, but otherwise he felt as if his own life was useless and of no consequence because he had no heir to follow him.

It was then, as Georgina grew older, she became in fact exactly as she was expected to become.

Beautiful to look at and with a strong athletic body which she had inherited from her father, the Earl began to treat her as if she was a boy and the heir he so longed for.

Because it came so easily to his lips. he called her "George" and, as she grew older, she was treated not as his daughter but as his son.

While she was still in the nursery, she rode a pony that would have been considered suitable for a child twice her age.

When she was eight years old, she was put onto one of her father's horses and rode it astride. It seemed to come to her so naturally.

It was perhaps from that moment on that the Earl began to believe that she really was a boy.

He taught her to shoot and to swim even when the lake was very cold.

When she was older still, she rode with him on long journeys in weather no woman would ever have considered suitable.

When the Countess suggested that she should have a Governess, the Earl found Tutors who taught her exactly as if she had been a boy of the same age.

Older still and continuing to ride astride, she took part in the steeplechase that her father had arranged for his friends and neighbours.

Although she did not win the steeplechase, she did at least complete the course.

The Earl was congratulated by all and sundry on having such a sporting daughter.

When she was twelve, she would, if she had been a boy, have been sent to Eton, but, as she was obliged to stay at home, her father found Tutors who taught her the same subjects she would have learnt at School.

What was more the Earl insisted on her learning the languages of other countries, as he believed that only by speaking to people in their own tongue could one be able to understand and appreciate them properly.

At fifteen Georgina could speak fluently most of the languages of Europe. She was having a special teacher in Urdu in case she wished to go to India and Japanese too.

By now she was such a good rider that she could ride the same horses as her father rode and she could take them over the jumps on their private Racecourse.

She could shoot pheasants and other game almost as well as he could.

What she lacked, but she would not admit it, were friends of her own age and, although a certain number of his friends brought their sons to The Castle, the daughters were never invited.

Of course Lady Georgina was talked about in the County, but, as she never accepted an invitation from their neighbours and lived in her own world that was barred to strangers, her life revolved round her father.

As the Countess was unable to travel or even to go to London, the Earl made her as happy as he could at The Castle.

She would, if she felt well enough, come down to luncheon and take a great interest in what her husband and daughter had done during the morning.

She rested in the afternoon before tea at four-thirty in the drawing room and at six o'clock she retired to her own bedroom.

Naturally Georgina went to see her, but she found that her father's conversation was far more interesting than anything her mother had to say to her.

The Earl, before he inherited, had travelled a great deal around the world.

It was when Georgina was just sixteen that he first suggested they should pay a visit to Africa and then they would visit Egypt and Turkey.

By this time many of her teachers had told the Earl that she knew just as much as they did and if it had been possible and women were admitted, she should have gone to a University.

"She has a man's brain, my Lord," one teacher said, "and it will soon be hard for anyone to teach her anything she does not already know."

Because he thought it diplomatic, he added,

"In fact she is just as clever, my Lord, as you are yourself and no man could ask more of his – son."

As he spoke the last word, the teacher knew that he had made a mistake and quickly changed it to 'daughter'.

He had known instinctively by the expression on the Earl's face that what he wanted, above all things, was to have that particular compliment paid to his son.

The visit to Africa, which should have been a great success, was, however, a disaster.

The Earl contracted a foreign disease of the throat, which was to trouble him for the rest of his life and it was down to Georgina to not only nurse him but to take him home sooner than they had expected.

It was when they arrived back they found that the Countess had been upset by the winter weather, although she seldom went out in it.

She was under the doctor's orders to do as little as possible and above all she had to stay in bed.

Georgina moved from one patient to the other and she found them both difficult to talk to or entertain.

Her mother died unexpectedly one night and was found in the morning by her lady's maid.

But her father was not well enough to arrange the funeral or to invite the relations.

Because she was so well trained, Georgina found no difficulty in compiling a list of the relatives who should be informed of her mother's death. She ordered the coffin as well as arranging the burial ceremony that was to take place in the grounds.

Because it was the middle of winter and because few of the Earl's relatives had seen the Countess for a long time, not many took the long journey to The Castle.

The Countess's family lived in the far North and they wrote to say that it was impossible to come South at that moment and they could only send their condolences.

When finally the funeral took place, there was only a sprinkling of relatives and the mourners consisted mostly of the people on the estate and the inhabitants of the local villages that the Earl owned.

It was only when they went back to The Castle that Georgina realised she must take over the household and save her father from exerting himself.

She found it very interesting and not particularly a great burden. In fact, as she was aware herself, there was not usually enough for her to do.

When her father had run everything, like the rest of the staff, she had had to obey him, but now she could give her orders and they were dutifully carried out.

She made some alterations in the household, which she had often thought was out of date.

It was an unbelievable joy when her father was well enough for him to come down to meals and to talk to her as they had always conversed after dinner.

Because he was finding that his eyes were tired, he made Georgina read the newspapers to him and they had long discussions on political and social topics, which she found entrancing.

Neither she nor the Earl realised that what they were discussing and their points of view would certainly not have happened with any other girl of her age.

At eighteen Georgina was really lovely. She had her mother's perfect pink and white skin and her golden hair.

But because she was always dressed as a boy and behaved as a boy, it had always been cut very short.

Nevertheless, because it was naturally curly, it did not strike anyone as being strange or if it did they were too polite to say so.

That, of course, extended to the way she dressed.

As she was always riding astride or shooting with her father, it would have been almost impossible to wear a skirt and so she wore riding breeches.

She expected to be reprimanded, but her father said nothing when she dined with him dressed as a man and wore riding clothes during the day.

It was easy to tell his valet to provide her with new shirts and it was only a question of a year or two before her wardrobe consisted entirely of male attire.

Yet now she had to face the fact that she was alone and she was not certain of what lay ahead for her in the future.

As her father had now died, it was obvious that the next Earl of Langfield would take his place.

And as far as Georgina was concerned, she was not certain who that was or where he could be found.

She had informed all the relatives of her father's death and, as she expected, only a very few of them had come to the funeral.

The weather was very bad and, just as her mother had died near Christmas, her father had done the same and she could hardly blame them for staying away.

At the same time when most of them refused to come back to The Castle before they returned home, she realised that they thought her strange and anyway they had no wish to be involved in a discussion as to who was to become the next Earl of Langfield.

There was food and drink arranged in the drawing room, but she had been aware that the visitors who were enjoying it were mostly local farmers and tenants.

Georgina realised that she now had to find out who she would hand over The Castle to and be told where on the estate she could live.

The Dower House, which had not been lived in for years, was in a sad state of disrepair and she thought if she had to go and live there it could be made more comfortable if money was spent on it.

She was not yet certain how much it would cost and she had learnt from one of her father's surveyors that the roof needed a great deal doing to it and most of the rooms required repainting.

She had intended at one time to look at the house, although it had never struck her until now that she perhaps would have to live in it.

But she had been so busy with the horses and with a great number of other matters that had to be dealt with in her father's absence.

It was only now that she had time to think about herself.

In fact because she had lived so exclusively at The Castle and, because in all the years of her life it had been the one place she knew so well, it was terrifying to realise that now she would have to go away.

'But where can I go?' she asked herself.

She knew that The Castle and the land round it had filled her whole life and been her world ever since she was old enough to think.

She was sensible enough to realise that her father had not only thought of her as a boy and let her dress as one but he had also made certain that she spent her time only with men.

His friends, her Tutors and the majority of servants like his Managers and his secretaries were the people she talked to and the people she knew.

It was only now that she realised that, if she paid a visit to a farmer on the estate, his wife would look at her shyly because of the way she was dressed.

Therefore she usually left them alone and the same applied to the neighbours who had long given up inviting her to their parties and she only came into contact with them when they were invited to The Castle.

Looking back, she saw that her father had treated her exclusively as if she was his son.

He gave her orders which she was expected to obey immediately.

She rode with him, went out shooting with him and fished in the streams where there were small trout.

It was a general rule that almost from first thing in the morning until late in the evening she was with him.

There were always situations to be seen to over the estate and she had been to numerous Horse Fairs with her father.

As she was always dressed as a boy, instinctively anyone who spoke to her called her 'sir'.

It was only now that Georgina was wondering if she should remain as a pseudo young man or become, as she felt she really ought to, a girl.

She was nearly twenty.

When she thought it over, she had done nothing in the past few years that was in the least feminine.

Looking back, she would find herself talking to her father's friends, who were inevitably men he had known since childhood. They talked mostly of their possessions in the country, although occasionally they would discuss the political situation.

Georgina had listened to them and found that what they were saying was extremely interesting, but she had known at the back of her mind that they were treating her as a boy and not a girl.

They were often rather embarrassed by her situation in the house and the way she was dressed.

'I suppose now that Papa is dead,' she thought, 'I will have to change myself into someone very different. But I really don't know how to do it.'

Once again she was thinking whether she would be allowed to stay on the estate, even if she could afford to repair the Dower House.

But, if she did live there, could she really bear to see someone else giving orders to the staff when she had always given them?

Perhaps what had mattered so much to her father would be either altered or neglected. More important still would anyone living at The Castle and knowing about her position there want her to watch them making alterations and perhaps being uncomfortably inquisitive?

'What am I to do? What on earth am I to do?' she asked herself again and for the first time in her life she was afraid of the future.

It was then that she heard the wheels of a carriage.

She thought that it must be someone leaving, who had been partaking of refreshments in the dining room.

She had seen, when she returned from the funeral, that there were only a few carriages outside the front door.

She had stayed behind after other people had left the Church to thank the Bishop, who had come to bury her father and she had also asked him if he would come up to The Castle before he left for home.

The Bishop had refused as he was so busy, but he had talked to her saying what a splendid man her father had been and how much he admired the work he had done on his estate.

The Bishop had been very charming and it was only at the end of the conversation he had said to Georgina,

"What are you going to do now, Lady Georgina? I realise that this must have been a terrible shock to you. I hope that you will be able to stay on at The Castle until you have decided where you will go."

Thinking of it now, she realised until that moment she had not actually considered where she should go and when.

For one thing she was not certain who the next heir would be. Her father had a great number of relatives he did not see from one year to the next and some of them lived in the very South of England.

Others lived abroad and there were some of the family in Scotland, but, because he had been pre-occupied with his enormous estate and his invalid wife, the Earl had made little effort to keep in touch with his large family.

Because it hurt him to think that he had no son to take his place, he had deliberately not calculated who, amongst his cousins, was the prospective heir.

Also, because he had not thought of dying while he was comparatively young, he was certain that Georgina would be married long before there was any need to look for an heir.

He was determined not to lose her companionship until he absolutely had to, as she was the son he never had.

Her companionship and her interest in everything he said and did made her much more indispensable in his daily life than even his son might have been.

'What can I do now,' Georgina asked herself, 'to find out who is taking Papa's place and whether he will want my help or just be glad to be rid of me?'

She was apprehensive of the answer.

She crossed the room to look once again at the big pile of letters on her father's desk. The servants had put them there as they arrived, knowing that she would deal with them when she had the time.

She was sure that many of the letters would need a reply, but she had no wish to read them yet. They could wait just as she was having to wait to learn of her own future.

Now she thought about it, she realised, as far as she was aware, that there had been no family relations at all in the Church.

However, there had been quite a number of people and it was impossible for her to be certain of who they all were, as she supposed that the Deacon or someone who had been at the door would have told any relatives to join her in the family pew.

But she had been alone during the Service and then, when the coffin had been carried to the family vault, she had gone with it.

With the sole exception of the Parson and the men carrying the coffin, there had been no one else.

'One cannot blame them,' she thought, 'because the weather was so bad.'

At the same time she was sure that her father would have been deeply hurt at the lack of interest his relatives were showing him.

'What I have to do now,' Georgina said to herself, 'is to see how much money I have left and make certain what in the house is mine.'

She shuddered at the idea.

But her father's Solicitor had written to say that he would call the day after the funeral to discuss her father's will with her.

She had no idea what he had said or what he had given her.

The one subject they had never discussed was what would happen to her in the future and she knew that it was because her father had no intention of dying yet.

There was no reason why he should have died if he had not caught that very unpleasant disease of the throat while he was in Africa.

Although they had visited the same places and been together all the time, she had been fortunate enough to remain well and healthy.

'I suppose that I should read these letters,' she told herself, 'instead of worrying myself and asking questions I have no answer to.'

She walked towards the desk and, as she did so, she was aware that there were voices coming from the hall.

She was surprised that it was a woman's voice she could hear above the rest and, as far as she had noticed, there had been no woman in the dining room where the refreshments were laid out.

There had certainly been no female relative at the funeral and the voice, talking animatedly, grew louder.

Georgina now realised that someone with a great deal to say was coming towards the study.

She wondered who on earth it could be. If it was someone local, she felt that they had no right to impose themselves on her at such a time and anyway she could not understand why the butler had not sent them away.

Dawson, who had been at The Castle ever since she could remember, would never allow a stranger to impose on her at this delicate moment.

The men who had come to her father's funeral and doubtless lived locally would have left without coming to The Castle, knowing that she would be the only person there and would naturally be exceedingly upset.

The voice grew louder still.

Then, as the door opened, Georgina saw a woman she did not for the moment recognise.

She was elegantly dressed in black with a feather hat and cape trimmed with black fur.

"Lady Crawford, my Lady," Dawson announced in a stentorian voice.

Then a vision in black pushed past him into the room and for a moment Georgina could only stare at the newcomer with astonishment.

Then the shrill voice she had heard in the passage piped up,

"My dear Georgina, how can I apologise enough! But we had a breakdown on the road and by the time the wheel was repaired the Service was over. I am so sorry, so very sorry to have missed saying my last prayers for your dear father."

It was with an effort that Georgina realised that it was her aunt, who had not been to The Castle for many years, although she had often written to her father.

"It is so kind of you to come," she managed to say.

"Of course we would come today," Lady Crawford replied, "and now here is Vivien, my daughter, and my son, Edward."

Vivien, a somewhat plain girl, was dressed in black too and she shook hands with Georgina without saying anything.

Her brother, however, who must have been about eighteen, said rather uncomfortably,

"I am sorry we were not present at the funeral."

"We did our best," Lady Crawford explained, "but it was impossible to move until the wheel was repaired and you know what local people are like. They could not hurry if the sky was falling in!"

Before Georgina could reply, she looked round the room and said,

"Oh dear, I remember this room. Nothing changes and I always thought that The Castle was such an exciting romantic place."

As if she knew instinctively what Georgina would ask her, Lady Crawford went on,

"Last time I came here was soon after you were born. Your father asked me and my husband to a dinner party."

She gave a laugh before she added,

"He did not realise until we arrived here that we expected to stay the night. He was quite astonished when I told him that I had no intention of driving back such a long distance in the dark."

Georgina found her tongue and realised that there was a point to this story.

Then she asked,

"Would you like to stay tonight as you have come such a long way, Aunt Marjory?"

"That is very kind of you, dear," Lady Crawford replied. "We hoped that you would be generous enough to invite us. I have told my children all about The Castle and they are longing to explore it. I felt sure that you would be able to squeeze us in."

"There is no one else staying," Georgina replied. "In fact because the weather has been so bad the majority of the family, who as you know live mostly in London or in the South, were not able to be at the funeral."

"Oh dear, I had hoped to see our relatives," Lady Crawford said. "It's so seldom we get together and your father has been very reluctant, I feel, to arrange much in the last five years or so."

She settled herself comfortably on the sofa, saying,

"I hope you don't mind, but I told your butler I was very thirsty and longing for something to drink."

As she spoke, the door opened and Dawson came in followed by a footman carrying a tray. They set it down on the table which stood near the window.

Georgina, thinking that things had really been taken out of her hands, did not speak while her unexpected guests were given glasses of champagne.

"This is so kind, so very very kind of you!" Lady Crawford gushed. "Of course we expected to find a large number of the family here who I really wanted to see."

Thinking she had already answered that question, Georgina asked,

"I was wondering before you arrived who inherits the title now that Papa is dead."

Lady Crawford stared at her.

"But, of course, I know. That actually is why I am here to talk to you about him."

"But who is he?" Georgina enquired. "It seems so strange, but it is something my father never told me."

Lady Crawford stared at her again.

"That is odd, very odd. He must have known or perhaps he did not want you to know about Alister."

Georgina gazed at her.

"Who are you talking about?" she asked.

She was thinking as she spoke if she had ever heard of a relative of her father's called Alister, but she was almost certain that he had never spoken of one.

"You don't know?" Lady Crawford asked. "That is extraordinary! Then I have a great deal to tell you."

Georgina waited still wondering who Alister could be and why she had not heard of him.

After a large sip of the champagne, Lady Crawford went on,

"I think perhaps we will leave this until later. At the moment I am so delighted that we can stay here with you. I know my dear children want to explore The Castle. I have told them so much about it. Is that right, dears?"

She turned to the children rather affectedly as she spoke and the boy replied,

"You have talked about it, Mama, all the way here and you will doubtless talk about it all the way back."

Lady Crawford gave a little cry.

"Oh, you naughty boy! That is not the sort of thing you should say to me in front of our relative. Now, as you have lots of time before dinner, you and Vivien can go and explore the music room, which I remember particularly and I am sure it's as beautiful as it was when I was your age."

Her two children realising that they were dismissed, rose to their feet holding their glasses of champagne in their hands.

The boy, however, walked to the table and filled his glass to the top and then he said,

"I am sure we will get lost if it is anything like you have been describing to us, Mama. So, if we don't appear at dinner, you might send a footman to find us."

Lady Crawford laughed.

"Go on, you impudent boy, and don't forget to look at the library. I have told you it's famous for its collection of books and I only hope that you will read some of them. It will do you good."

"Well, don't finish all the champagne before we come back," Edward remarked as he walked to the door.

"Go on, you cheeky boy," she replied. "Don't hurry as I have much to say to dear Georgina."

Edward and Vivien left the room and as they closed the door Lady Crawford drank more of her champagne.

Then she said,

"I suppose, my dear Georgina, you know all about who will take your father's place and who it is who now becomes the eleventh Earl of Langfield."

CHAPTER TWO

Georgina was trying to recall what she had heard about Alister, but for the moment her mind was completely blank.

Then Lady Crawford went on,

"Now let's sit down, dear. I have so much to tell you and I want you to listen attentively to me."

Georgina smiled.

"Yes, of course, Aunt Marjory. But you have not been here for many years."

"Yes, I know, dear, but I recognised that it would upset your father if I came to see him simply because I had three sons and he had none."

Georgina realised this was true and it embarrassed her too because she knew her father had so wanted a boy.

Lady Crawford finished her champagne and then she burbled on,

"Now listen because it is important that you should do so."

"I have been wondering," Georgina mused, "when I last saw Alister Lang. Surely he is not a close cousin."

"I want to start at the beginning," Lady Crawford told her. "As you know your father was the only son and his parents had one daughter, who was me."

Georgina knew all this and wondered why her aunt was making such a fuss about it.

"The one thing our father drummed into us almost as soon as we were born," Lady Crawford went on, "was that our name was one of the most ancient of all lineages in British history and it was so essential that the Langs should have plenty of sons to carry on the name into the future."

Georgina gave a sigh.

She knew this and had heard it often, but towards the end of his life, she had been careful not to let her father talk about who would take his place when he died.

In fact she had no idea that he would die so young or so unexpectedly and they had not discussed the Family Tree for at least three or four years.

"It was when I heard your father was ill when you came back from Africa," Lady Crawford continued, "that I realised he had paid very little attention to the Family Tree, which had always been so close to his heart."

"I had no idea that Papa was so bad or that he would die of that terrible disease," Georgina replied.

"I think it was lucky you did not catch it, but my husband and I are aware how dangerous these diseases can be in Africa. We were therefore apprehensive as to what would happen to my dear brother."

There was a distinct note of sincerity in her voice that Georgina had felt was missing when she had talked of her brother before.

She therefore listened more attentively to what her aunt was saying.

"It was my husband who worked out, with quite some difficulty I may say, that the direct heir was, in fact, Alister, and we had not heard of him for some time."

"Why? Where is he?" Georgina enquired.

"You may well ask. He disappeared some years earlier and had not kept in touch with any of the family."

"I am now trying to remember what I know about Alister. In fact I only met him once or twice when he was still a boy."

"That is very likely true," Lady Crawford agreed. "I can quite understand your father having no wish to see him here taking the place of the son he never had."

"Oh, poor Papa, he was very sad that I was his only child," Georgina sighed.

"It was a disaster. It was when he learnt that your mother could not have any more children that he began to shut himself away from the family. He just spent his time with you."

Lady Crawford turned to look at Georgina as she spoke, who was aware that she was disapproving of her clothes and her whole appearance.

However, as she knew that the family objected to her looking like a boy, she enquired quickly,

"Tell me more about Alister, Aunt Marjory."

"He is now on his way home. After a great deal of trouble my husband and I found he was living in Japan."

"Japan!" Georgina exclaimed in amazement. "Why should he want to go there?"

She thought that her cousin, if that was who Alister was, would have wanted to enjoy the amusements of Paris, Vienna and the other Cities of Europe or maybe he wanted to climb mountains as her father had done in his youth.

"Alister went to Japan," her aunt replied, speaking slowly and positively, "because the women there are very soft, sweet and gentle and obedient to their menfolk."

She saw surprise in Georgina's eyes and went on,

"Surely your father told you about him and what happened when he married."

"Perhaps Papa did do so," Georgina answered, "but I cannot remember what he said."

"Well, I will make it very clear to you because that is why I am here. Alister married when he was very young. In point of fact he was only twenty-one. This was because a great deal of pressure was put on him to propose to the daughter of the Duke of Atherton."

She paused before continuing,

"She was a very pretty girl and as both parents were so keen on the union they were, in my opinion, pushed into it almost before they knew what was happening."

Georgina was listening intently to her, as she was now sure that she had not been told about this before.

"Alice came from a very ancient and very respected family. We were all very aware that it was unlikely your mother would be able to have another child."

Georgina thought she could hear it all happening and she was certain the family had made the two people concerned feel that they must marry each other. There was really no chance of them being able to refuse.

"They were married at the Duke's house in Kent," Lady Crawford was saying. "All the family attended with the exception of your father and, of course, your mother who was not well enough to do so."

"Why did Papa not go?" Georgina asked.

"I am sure, although he did not say so, he was well aware that Alister was his heir. But he was still hoping that by some miracle he would be able to have a son to take his place when he died."

Georgina could not help thinking that, if her mother had died sooner, there would have been a chance of her father marrying again.

Although she was really nothing but an invalid, she had still been looking lovely but quite incapable of playing any part in anything.

"We all thought that Alister was really in love with his wife, who was a very good-looking girl, except that she had a rather hard face and an abrupt way of talking."

"But he loved her?" Georgina enquired.

"I think he did at first or perhaps when he actually proposed. But, once they were married, they disagreed on every subject. He found that she was very different from what he expected of his bride."

"You mean that she was aggressive?"

"She was indeed aggressive and determined to have her own way whether right or wrong. We were actually told, secretly of course, that they quarrelled every day from dawn to dusk."

"I cannot understand why," Georgina said.

"The reason was quite simple. Alister's wife was one of those modern, pushy and up to date women who consider themselves equal if not superior to men."

Georgina laughed.

"I thought that they only existed in books or in the newspapers."

"They exist alright and, of course, a great number of men, with Alister amongst them, disapprove of Queen Victoria reigning alone instead of, after Prince Albert died, taking another Prince Consort to help her."

"And to share the throne," Georgina remarked. "I can understand in a way why Her Majesty not only refused to marry but has not allowed the Prince of Wales to take any part in State Affairs."

"Alister considers it disgraceful and incidentally so does my husband," Lady Crawford said. "In fact you will find that most men believe women should stay in their rightful place which naturally is the home."

"I have often thought when I heard about it that, as they have been badly treated for many years, it is obvious that, now with Queen Victoria's example in front of them, they will want to rebel," Georgina commented.

Her aunt held up her hands in horror.

"You must not talk like that! That is exactly why I have come here today to see you!"

Georgina stared at her.

"Are you saying that I should not be sorry for the women who are downtrodden and who have to obey a man whatever he tells them to do?" she questioned.

"Of course that is how women should behave," her aunt replied, "especially someone in your position."

She spoke in such a positive way that Georgina looked at her in surprise.

"My position?" she queried.

"Now listen first to what I have to tell you," Lady Crawford went on. "I must finish my story. Alister found his wife intolerable and so he left her after they had been married for only a few months."

"He left her!" Georgina exclaimed.

"He left her and went abroad. He travelled to all sorts of strange countries and made it clear that he had no intention of returning."

"I have never heard this before," Georgina replied.

"Of course because the Duke, her father, was so important, he made certain that it was not known outside the family. Alister's wife said that he had gone abroad on a vital mission and the family backed her up because the last thing they wanted was a scandal."

"I can understand that," Georgina mused. "But it must have been strange if he was away for a long time."

"He was abroad from the time he married until now when he is returning," Lady Crawford informed her. "In fact he is now twenty-nine and has not been in England for eight years."

Georgina was intrigued.

"What was he doing all the time? Surely his wife asked him to return."

"If she did, he ignored it. He was out of touch with the family for the simple reason that they had no idea of where he was and the world is a big place."

Georgina chuckled.

"It's the funniest story I have ever heard, all of this because he argued with her."

"She not only argued, but she was aggressive and insisted that she was right and that he was wrong."

"Perhaps he was," Georgina retorted.

Her aunt gave another cry of horror.

"You must not think like that! You must realise now your father is dead that you have to obey, as we all do, the new Head of the Family."

"And if I do not?" Georgina asked.

"Then you will find it very difficult to live without money," Lady Crawford replied.

Georgina stared at her.

"What do you mean – without money?"

"I see your father must have kept you very ignorant of what occurs in all great families and especially in ours," Lady Crawford said sharply.

"Then explain to me what you mean!"

"The Head of the Family, who for us is the reigning Earl, is responsible for looking after all his relations and giving each one of them what he can afford."

She took a deep breath as she went on,

"Some of them of course, if they are women, have married into money and are therefore not so dependent on him as for instance I am."

Georgina stared at her.

"I don't understand!" she exclaimed.

"Well, let me make it clear. My husband, although he has a very delightful house and a title, was the second son. Therefore he had very little to bless himself with."

She shook her head as she rambled on,

"But we have a house that is large and comfortable and plenty of horses for our children who have all been educated at the best schools. This was entirely thanks to your father who, as Head of the Family, gave me a very generous allowance from the time I grew up."

Georgina was listening intently.

"The same applies to a large number of the family who are entirely dependent on what they received from your father. They will now be dependent on Alister."

"I had no idea of this," Georgina said. "We always seemed to have plenty of money."

"Of course *you* had plenty of money. Your father was a very rich man. Your mother also had a considerable amount of money which I understand she left in her will to your father knowing that he would provide for you."

"I knew that Mama's father was rich and I always thought that what money she had she would leave to me," Georgina replied in a small voice.

"My husband discussed it all with your father's Solicitor yesterday and discovered, as I think he expected, that your father obeyed the unwritten laws of those who are proud of their ancestry which was that the reigning Duke, Marquis or Baron are 'Fathers' of what the Scots would call 'the Clan'. Each one of them has to rely on him for their existence."

There was silence for a while before Georgina said,

"What you are saying, Aunt Marjory, is that I own nothing and have to beg my cousin Alister for every penny I need."

She spoke very slowly as if she was thinking it out for herself.

"Yes, that is true, but, of course, your mother has left you her jewellery and a number of other items, which I should have thought she would have discussed with you."

"No, she did not discuss it," Georgina answered. "Strangely enough Papa never mentioned it when she died. I have never worn jewellery and what belonged to Mama was put away in a safe and I did not think of taking it out."

"Well, I should take it out now because it's yours. At the same time you must be very pleasant and obedient to anything that your cousin Alister asks of you."

"I thought of asking him if he did not want me in The Castle, if I could have the Dower House. But perhaps I would be wise to go away. But where to, I have no idea."

"That would be a disaster for all of us," her aunt replied sharply. "You have to stay here and make yourself indispensable to Alister, so he will listen to what you say. He will then understand how dependent we all are on him."

She made a gesture with her hands and went on,

"Heaven knows if he has any idea at all of what has happened here in England as he has been away so long. I am certain that he had no idea he would become Head of the Family."

"But suppose he will not listen to me?" Georgina enquired.

"That is what we are afraid of," her aunt replied. "It is why I wanted to see you today immediately after the funeral and before Alister arrives."

She spoke so seriously that Georgina stared at her,

"We were all aware when your father was so ill that if he did die the only person who could help us was you. You will therefore have to make Alister listen to you."

"But suppose he will not," Georgina asked.

"Then you are condemning us to a future which is unbearable to think about," Lady Crawford retorted with a sniff.

Then in a quieter voice she went on,

"Surely you understand that, as everything depends on *you*, we have to beg you to consider the plight we will be in. If Alister does not understand because he has been away so long what his position is as the eleventh Earl of Langfield and the Head of the Family, one that has been admired and respected in this country for generations, then you must force him to understand!"

"I appreciate your feelings, but, if Alister does not like me, there will be nothing I can do about it."

"You have to make him like you," her aunt said firmly. "That is why I have come to tell you from the family that you have to change your ways and become a very different woman from the one you are now."

"Change my ways?" Georgina questioned.

"Don't be so silly! You must be aware that dressing up as a boy and pretending to be a boy might have pleased your father, but to us it is a complete and utter disaster and will be to Alister too."

"You mean Cousin Alister will be shocked?"

31

"Not only shocked, but you may drive him away as his wife did. If he disappears out into the world as he has done before, we might even starve because of his absence."

There was a long silence before Georgina said in a voice that sounded very different from her own.

"What do you want me to do?"

"Now you are talking more sense and realising your responsibilities. Of course the answer to your question is obvious. First you have to behave like a woman and the sort of woman that Alister admires, which, as we already know, is soft, sweet and gentle."

Georgina stared at her.

"That is something I suppose I have never been and have no idea what I should do."

"That is what I have come to tell you," her aunt replied. "I assure you that we have all been very shocked for a long time at the way your father treated you as if you were a boy and made you look like one."

"It is the way I have always been – "

"Yes, we have all thought it disgraceful, I can tell you. I don't know how many times I have had to pretend to strangers that it was because your father was so unhappy that he could not have a son that his wife and you made him happy by pretending you were one."

She gave a laugh with no humour in it as she added,

"Most people thought we were crazy. Frankly it was what I always thought you were."

"I suppose because Papa had treated me as if I was a son ever since I was born," Georgina answered her, "I have never thought about it. I loved riding and shooting with Papa and discussing the estate and because we did everything in every sort of weather it was easier to wear boy's clothes than the frills and furbelows of a girl."

"Well, that is what you must have now, because we all realise that there was little time for you to go shopping even if you knew the right things to buy, so I have brought with me a selection of clothes which I am sure you will find delightful once you have put them on."

Georgina put her hand up to her forehead as if she found it difficult to understand what was being said.

Then unexpectedly she laughed.

"This just cannot be true!" she exclaimed. "You are telling me I have to change in twenty-four hours from being what I have always been and become very feminine. And I don't think that I will be able to play that part at all successfully."

"If you don't, we will all starve," Lady Crawford cried angrily, "so get that into your head! Now we are going upstairs and I want you to transform yourself in the beautiful clothes I have brought. I want you to change the rather scruffy young boy into a pretty, soft, tender, alluring woman."

She was speaking so seriously and again Georgina laughed.

"This cannot be real! It cannot be happening to me and I know I will make a mess of it."

"You will do nothing of the sort," her aunt said. "We never stopped being told by your father how clever you are, how many languages you speak and how every Tutor would have given you a certificate if it had been in his power."

"Papa certainly wanted me to be intelligent," she agreed. "But now I am afraid that I am too intelligent to be a successful and subservient woman."

"If you have any intelligence at all you will realise it is absolutely essential that you should be," her aunt went on. "Therefore the sooner we get to work the better."

"But how can you be certain, as you have not seen him for so long, that Alister still hates women who have brains?" Georgina asked.

"That is the sort of question you should not ask as a woman. If you have any brains then acting out what you really are should not be difficult as long as you don't assert yourself or in any way show that you don't consider a man as a superior being to a woman."

Georgina rose and walked across the room to the writing desk.

It was almost as if she expected her father to be sitting there and then she would discuss some difficulty on the estate with him.

She would firmly express her opinion as to what should be done, knowing that he would listen attentively and they would finally work out together what was the best way to put matters right.

She had read enough books and magazines to know that women were beginning to assert themselves as they had never done before. If Queen Victoria, they said, could rule over a third of the world and Britain could lead the way and intimidate every other nation, then women should take their rightful place in Society.

And they should also be acknowledged as having in their own way the same standing as men.

Her father had often criticised the fact that women were pushing themselves forward in a number of ways that he thought unbecoming to their sex.

He had in fact been very much against Florence Nightingale going out in the Crimean war with a team of nurses. It had never happened previously and some people believed that it would end in disaster. That she had come back triumphant with an acknowledged success had made him refuse to talk about her again.

It was only through the reports in the newspapers, which she did not show to her father, that Georgina was aware that because of Florence Nightingale nursing gained a reputation it had never had before.

There were articles in the newspapers suggesting that women should play a greater part in the education of children and in fact they should come out of the home and into the world that was ruled entirely by men.

Georgina knew exactly what her father's answer to such questions would be and so she prevented herself from mentioning it.

She could understand in a way that Alister, having run away from his wife because she opposed him, would not tolerate any woman interfering with him in the future.

Because she was thinking it out, she asked aloud,

"Why did Alister's wife die? I was not told about it, but I gather from what you said that she has died."

"She died four years after he left her and it was the sort of death one could expect from a woman who asserted herself to such an extent that her husband ran away."

"What happened?" Georgina asked.

"She bought, in Alister's absence, some horses at a local sale which were known to be high-spirited. Actually they had been badly broken in."

"Then why did she buy them?"

"Because she wanted to assert herself," was the reply. "Several men, including my husband, advised her they were not a good buy and that she would not be able to handle them."

"But, of course, it was a challenge?" Georgina said enquiringly.

"Exactly. She bought the horses and on the first report we were told it had been an excellent buy and the horses had completely changed since she had become their owner. They were, of course, highly bred to start with. It was only through mismanagement that they had grown out of control and thus a danger."

"So what happened?" Georgina asked.

"You can guess the answer to that. Teaching one of the worst of them to jump, he threw her and rolled on top of her. Several of her ribs were broken and she died a fortnight after the accident."

Georgina sighed.

"So everyone said it was because she was trying to assert herself," she murmured.

"Of course they did," Lady Crawford agreed. "She was, in everyone's opinion, quite unnecessarily doing a man's job and therefore deserved the consequences."

Georgina sighed again.

"Poor woman, I feel rather sorry for her."

"You need not be. It was entirely her fault that she drove Alister away and her fault that he has been out of touch with the family until now."

"It must have been clever of your husband to find him," Georgina remarked.

"Very clever. In fact we spent a great deal of money sending people to look for him in different parts of the world where we had heard vaguely that at one time or another he had been seen."

"And you eventually found him in Japan?"

Lady Crawford nodded.

"He was in Japan with the entrancing and very feminine Japanese women!"

"Do you honestly think that I can play the same part for him and at the same time help him on the estate?" Georgina asked.

"The estate is excellent, as my husband learnt when he made enquiries, it is not only paying its way but making a large profit compared to your grandfather's time."

Georgina smiled.

"Papa was so interested in farming. He put forward new ideas that have helped the farmers enormously."

"That is another thing which I am sure will interest Alister when he arrives," Lady Crawford told her. "But you have to be very clever to prevent him sending you away immediately as he might do especially if he saw you as you look now."

"I will do what I can," Georgina murmured, "but I cannot promise that I will be successful."

"You have to be!" her aunt said firmly. "We are all depending on you. If you heard how everyone deplored the manner in which you have been brought up by your father, you would now welcome us when we offer you the chance of becoming what you were meant to be, a pretty, tactful and charming woman."

Georgina laughed.

"It's no use, Aunt Marjory, you know I will never be that. But I promise you I will try very hard."

"Well, after the excellent education you have had from the most distinguished and expensive Tutors in the country," Lady Crawford retorted, "I should have thought that you would find nothing impossible."

Georgina wanted to argue that what she had learnt from her Tutors had been the lessons that a boy would have enjoyed.

The knowledge she had gained would have been of great help to a man.

Now, she thought, to change herself completely into a woman was worse than any examination she had ever taken and the result, as far as she could see, would be one of complete failure.

"Now what we have to do," Lady Crawford was saying, "is go upstairs to your room where you will find what I have already had unpacked for you. We will throw away those ugly boy's clothes you are wearing at the moment."

With difficulty Georgina prevented herself from protesting that would be unnecessary and an extravagance.

Then she told herself that in her new role she must be subservient and appear to have no mind of her own.

They therefore walked out of the study in silence up the passage where her father had hung the pictures and had positioned the furniture.

From the first moment anyone came through the front door they were impressed with what they saw and Georgina had helped him arrange the other rooms so that the furniture and the pictures were of the same period as each other.

In fact even when she was quite young, Georgina had learnt a great deal of history from the possessions of The Castle.

Her father had made the library one of the finest and largest in the County and, when a new history book or the memoirs of a great man became available, they would read it together.

The Earl had expected Georgina to express her opinion on all that they said and what they had done.

So it was not surprising that, as she and her aunt climbed the stairs, she was wondering if her cousin Alister would expect her, if anything was wrong, to prevent herself from mentioning it.

Georgina's room on the first floor was an especially beautiful one and she had moved into it to be close to her father.

It boasted a large canopied four-poster bed, which was one of the treasures of The Castle and her boudoir was furnished with exquisite French furniture that had been brought over to England after the Revolution.

However, as she opened the door, she was unable to speak.

Lying on the bed, hanging from every wardrobe and over every chair, even on the window seats, there were gowns.

There were so many that for the moment Georgina was speechless.

Her aunt laughed.

"I thought you would be surprised. Every member of the family has contributed what they could spare. Even if they wanted to keep them, they felt they were giving to a good cause!"

"But I will never wear all these dresses!" Georgina exclaimed.

"You will," her aunt answered smiling. "And you will soon say that you have nothing to wear and be asking for more! That is what every woman is expected to do and will, of course, be your guideline from now on."

As she spoke, Lady Crawford moved over to where there was a large trunk lying on the floor.

She opened it and Georgina saw that it contained all the underclothes she would require if she was to become a woman.

She could not prevent herself shuddering when she saw the tight-laced bodice that she knew every fashionable woman wore under her gown and it was an article she had never possessed.

There were countless underclothes made of silk and embellished with real lace that she remembered her mother had always bought.

There were also silk stockings, high-heeled shoes and pairs of long kid gloves the like of which had never graced her arms.

"Because I thought it would embarrass you," her aunt was saying, "I told the maids not to come here until you rang for them. So change your clothes now and let's be rid of those hideous trousers once and for all."

"No, I will keep them," Georgina breathed, "so that I can remember the happy days when I was free to be myself. But now because you insist on it, Aunt Marjory, I am going to act the part of a woman for which I have no talent and practically no knowledge!"

"You will soon learn and I promise, if you persuade your cousin to invite us to stay here, we will be only be too delighted to accept."

"Oh, please," Georgina insisted. "It would be much better if you were here when he arrived."

"We thought that over, but we decided it might be overwhelming for him to meet too many of the family at once. After all he has managed quite well without us all these years."

She glanced at Georgina before she continued,

"Although we have no wish to impose on him, it is entirely up to you to make him realise that we utterly and completely depend on him."

"I should have thought that would make him run away even quicker than he did the first time," Georgina replied with a twinkle in her eyes.

Her aunt gave a cry.

"That is the sort of answer that a soft, sweet and gentle woman would not make to anyone, especially to a man!"

Because she found it funny, Georgina laughed.

"I don't think that I am going to make a very good woman."

"Good or bad you are going to be a woman and you *must* be clever and subtle with Alister."

Quite suddenly her aunt's face altered completely and she said angrily,

"Now listen to me. You have been told over and over again how clever you are, how if you were a boy you would have achieved a First at Oxford and doubtless made your mark in the House of Lords. Was that all lies?"

"No, it was true. But that did not teach me how to persuade a man who apparently does not like women to do what I want."

"Does not like women?" her aunt questioned her, her voice rising as she spoke. "Of course he likes women, but he likes them to be women and not pseudo-men as you have been!"

"What you are saying is that he wants someone without brains and idiotic enough to do exactly what he says without asking any questions."

"Now you are really talking nonsense!" her aunt exclaimed. "Of course that is what every man wants. But don't forget that the woman has to look beautiful, her skin has to be as white as snow and her main job in life is to entrance and delight a man."

"For that composition," Georgina retorted, "I will get no marks and doubtless have to wear a dunce's cap."

"If that is true, then what they have said about you has been lies from beginning to end."

Georgina did not answer and she went on,

"If you are half as clever as your father thought you to be then, of course, you could not only win the Battle of Waterloo as a man," Lady Crawford insisted, "but as a woman you can captivate the heart of any man who looks at you especially one who is determined not to be deceived for the second time by a pretty face."

Georgina clapped her hands.

"That is a splendid resumé of what I now have to attempt, Aunt Marjory, and I never knew that you were so clever or, if it suited, you could speak like a man."

"Now you are deliberately turning the tables on me for your own ends. I know exactly what you are thinking, but quite seriously you *have* to help us."

She sounded more worried as she continued,

"We are terribly afraid that Alister, because he has been abroad for so long, has no idea of his situation in England or how important he has now become because he is an Earl."

"I would expect he will learn that quickly enough," Georgina replied. "Then he will doubtless show me the front door."

"Well, I can offer you a bed in a very small room," her aunt suggested. "My house is not nearly as large as The Castle, but unless you are very stupid, which I find hard to believe after all I have heard about your brilliance, you will make Alister open the London house which your father closed up. It has stood in Grosvenor Square looking very sad and unused for years."

"I had actually forgotten all about it!" Georgina exclaimed. "Papa did mention it once or twice, but, as he had no wish to go to London and I was so happy with him here, we did not talk about it again."

"Well, you must do something about it now. It would suit the family and there are a great number of us who would like somewhere to stay when we visit London rather than having to go to an expensive hotel or beg a bed from one of our friends."

"So that is another thing I have to do," Georgina answered. "I think it would be wise if you make a list of them."

"You will find them all out sooner or later."

Then, as she saw that Georgina had dressed herself in some of the underclothes and was now staring at the wardrobe, she said,

"I suppose you know that your bodice is not nearly tight enough to be fashionable. Although I admit that you have a good figure, which must be due to all your riding."

"Although it kept my figure," Georgina remarked, "I am afraid that my feet are rather heavy in my shoes and, of course, I am not used to walking in heels."

"Then the sooner you learn the better! Now put on this gown and see what you look like in it."

Lady Crawford took out of the wardrobe a very pretty gown of pale pink, which was ornamented with lace and drawn at the back into a large bustle.

Georgina put it on and her aunt fastened it up.

As she sat gazing at her reflection in the mirror, she thought that she was a complete stranger and someone she had never seen before.

"Now that's better," her aunt was saying. "What a shame you had your hair cut short like a boy and, although it is naturally curly, it still looks rather scant, so I brought you a wig."

"*A wig!*"

"I think you will find that it is almost the right colour and certainly more becoming than your hair is now. You will find the wig in a box by the fireplace."

When she opened the box, Georgina laughed and pulled the wig rather roughly onto her head.

As she looked in the mirror again, she had to admit that she really was totally different.

Because the gown was meant for the evening, it showed how white her skin was and the wig with its soft curls on either side of her face was most becoming.

As if her aunt was thinking the same, she said,

"I have to admit, and I hope that Alister agrees, that you are now a very pretty girl."

Georgina chuckled.

"You may change my appearance, Aunt Marjory, but you cannot change my heart, which is undoubtedly that of a boy."

"Then you must never say so and you must stop thinking that way."

"I suppose the only thing I can do," she murmured, glancing again at herself in the mirror, "is to believe that this is entirely a game or even a steeplechase with a special prize at the end of it and I shall have to win!"

CHAPTER THREE

"Now you must change into an afternoon dress," Lady Crawford persisted.

"Change again!" Georgina exclaimed, "but that will be a bore and I am now ready for dinner."

"You are nothing of the sort! I want you to try some of the other clothes to be quite certain they fit you."

Because she had to wish to antagonise her aunt, Georgina agreed even though she thought that it was all a lot of nonsense.

She put on a pretty evening gown that her aunt said had only been worn twice by the previous owner.

She then changed again into what her aunt said was the right gown for tea and it was even lovelier than the one she had just taken off and it accentuated the whiteness of her skin and the fairness of her hair.

"Now you can keep that one on," Lady Crawford told her. "And you must put on your wig."

"I don't want to, it tickles the side of my face and would feel heavy as if I am wearing a hat."

"From now on," her aunt said firmly, "you are a very attractive woman. Women always look their best at teatime when they change into something clean and light. And what is more, you never know who will come in and see you."

"I imagine that they would be surprised to see me," Georgina laughed, "if I was wearing this dress and had my hair parted at the side and smoothed back as I wore it when I was a boy."

"You have never been a boy and so it's no use pretending that you were one," Lady Crawford retorted severely. "Your father had the absurd notion that he could turn you into a boy and now I am utterly and completely determined that I will make you what you were when you were born – a girl."

Georgina smiled

"It's going to be a struggle and will take a long time. What will happen if the new Earl arrives while I am changing?"

"If you make him horrified at what he finds, then he will go abroad again and I am quite certain his money will go with him."

Georgina realised that her aunt had the best of the argument and it was no use going on with it.

"Very well, I will try very hard for all your sakes, but, if he does run off, then you must all help me as I will have nowhere to go and apparently no money."

"If you let the estate go to ruin and The Castle fall down," her aunt warned, "I think when you are older you would never be able to forgive yourself."

"Do you really think that could happen?"

"I am certain of it. Who else, but a man who was really badly stricken, would disappear for so long and live in countries where there were not hard-faced, hard-tongued women pretending they were men?"

Because she spoke so sternly, Georgina laughed.

"Now you are really attacking me, Aunt Marjory," she protested, "and I have promised you I will do my best."

"I know you have, but you know we are all frantic in case Alister takes just one look at you and then leaves immediately for the Far East again."

"Do I really look as bad as all that?" she asked.

"You did when I arrived and you looked like a boy, except of course you do have a very pretty face."

"Now you are flattering me," Georgina said, "by making me think I will be a pretty girl. I am quite certain from the way I lived with Papa that I will always think like a boy and act like one. Although I will try not to show it, it will always be there just beneath the surface."

Although her aunt did not answer, she was thinking almost despairingly that matters were even worse than the rest of the family thought.

She walked across the room and stood looking out of the window and there was silence for a long time.

Then Georgina asked,

"Are you very angry with me?"

"I am not angry only rather apprehensive," her aunt replied. "I was remembering how proud and delighted we were when your father inherited the Earldom. We believed that this castle was something out of a dream."

"Which it is. I have often felt it myself."

"Then how can you bear to let it fall into rack and ruin and the people on the estate will starve if they cannot find other employment."

Georgina knew without her aunt explaining it how this was likely to happen.

The Earl of Langfield owned the land all round The Castle and she had very often thought it extraordinary how many people were employed by her father and how many families had lived on the estate for generations.

Suddenly she thought that she was being absurd in not doing exactly what her aunt wanted and frightening her by saying how incompetent she was.

She jumped up from the stool and joined her at the window.

"I am sorry, Aunt Marjory," she apologised. "I am just being tiresome and, of course, I will try to help you and you must all pray I don't make too many mistakes."

She now spoke in such a different voice that her aunt turned to look at her in surprise and remarked,

"I think you mean that."

"I do mean it! It has been such a shock with Papa dying and you telling me I have to be someone different, then Alister arriving from the far end of the world. It all seems so unreal!"

"Of course it does," Lady Crawford sympathised. "I know now that you are really one of us and will not let us down."

"I will try not to," Georgina promised.

Wearing her wig and the pretty dress her aunt had chosen for her, they went downstairs.

Dawson had already laid tea in the drawing room.

Her aunt, who would have sat down on the sofa and then picked up the silver teapot, stopped herself.

"You are the hostess, dearest," she reminded her, "and you must make it clear to Alister as soon as he arrives that, as he has no wife, you are prepared to run the house for him until he either marries or finds someone else."

"Suppose he asks me to leave at once – "

"I think that would be extremely rude. From what I remember of Alister, which is very little," Lady Crawford said, "I am sure that he will have the good manners to accept you in that position until he finds someone else."

Georgina only hoped that he would not do so too quickly.

She merely poured out the tea and helped herself to a sandwich and as she did so she realised that her hands did not show the whiteness of a woman who stayed in a house. They many had freckles on them and gave the appearance of belonging to someone who was frequently out of doors riding, fishing or shooting.

They certainly did not have the soft white skin of a woman.

"I must put something on my hands," she remarked. "I suppose they look rough because I don't wear gloves."

"You must wear them in the future," her aunt told her. "I will leave you some very good cream, which if you apply it every night will soon make your hands as white as the rest of your body."

She paused for a moment before she said,

"I was thinking how surprising it is that, although you have spent so much time out of doors, your skin is so white and not at all sunburnt. I am sure that the rest of the family expect you to look as if you are a gypsy rather than a young lady of fashion!"

Georgina giggled.

"Of course you are quite right. I have been out of doors with Papa day after day. I am only not sunburnt because I found it hurt me when my skin was exposed to the weather."

"Which it should not be because you have a very beautiful skin. You must take care of it and preserve it as every woman should do when she is given such a gift from Heaven."

"I did not think of it that way," Georgina replied. "But I promise I will in future."

When they finished tea, they went round the house and needless to say Lady Crawford made suggestions as to how nearly every room could be improved.

"I know that your father was so interested in being out of doors," she said, "that he forgot the house deserves just as much attention as the fields and the garden."

"There never seemed to be time for everything – "

"Well then, you must make it your business now to ensure that The Castle is as beautiful as it was when your mother first married. I remember how she was entranced by it and kept saying it was a fairy castle and she had no idea that anything like this really existed."

"I am sure she looked fairylike in it," Georgina replied, "which I will never do."

"Nonsense!" her aunt exclaimed. "You will look lovely once you think of yourself as being lovely and take trouble over it."

*

When she went up to bed, she announced,

"We are leaving early in the morning, as it is most important that I should not be here when Alister arrives. I have no idea when you can expect him. It may well be tomorrow or in two or three weeks."

"I do hope it's not tomorrow! I must get used to looking as I do now and I must make sure all the people on and around the estate recognise me."

Her aunt gave a little cry.

"I had not thought of that. Of course if they say, 'I had no idea it was you, my Lady,' then Alister will guess that you have changed from what you were and that would be a great mistake."

"I think I had better go round the main people on the estate," Georgina declared, "and explain to them that now Papa is dead I am going back to being what I was born – a girl."

"I think that is very sensible," her aunt agreed. "At the same time you don't want to make it too obvious that you are setting yourself out to please the new Earl, but rather returning to what you always wanted to be and what, of course, you were, a very pretty girl."

"I can see a lot of problems and difficulties ahead," Georgina murmured, "but I hope I will survive them."

"Of course you will. The one thing I have never disputed is that you have brains and brains are the one attribute in life that makes everything else possible."

Georgina laughed.

"Somehow I never expected you to say that to me, Aunt Marjory."

"Well, I have said it! And now you just have to be a very good girl and take care of the family as your father would want you to do."

*

The following morning when she kissed her niece goodbye Lady Crawford said quietly,

"I will be praying for you. At the same time that you will be successful and make Alister happy just as you made my brother happy."

Because she spoke with such feeling in her voice, Georgina could not reply.

She kissed her aunt again and her two cousins and then she waved until their carriage was out of sight.

As she walked back into the house, she saw that Dawson was waiting for her in the hall.

Because he had been at The Castle long before she was born, she knew that she could speak frankly to him.

She asked him to come into the study and, when he had done so, she asked him to close the door.

As she sat down at her father's desk, she began,

"I expect, Dawson, you are very surprised to see me dressed as I am."

"I were only sayin' to the Missus at breakfast this mornin' that, although you made a fine young gentleman, you makes an even finer lady. It's proud of you we all are but, of course, the housemaids have had a lot to say about you dressin' up as a boy for so long."

"I thought that would have happened, but you have to help me, Dawson, because, as I expect you will know, my cousin Alister was very unhappy in his marriage."

"It's not surprisin' from what I hears at the time, my Lady. His wife was a real fire-raiser, so to speak, and they quarrelled from the time they got up in the mornin' until they went to bed at night."

"I can understand why he went abroad, but it's very important to us all now he has returned that he should stay here."

"Yes, of course, my Lady, I understands that right enough. We'll all do our best to make him comfortable."

"I know you will. Equally Lady Crawford thinks it's essential he should not realise that my father dressed me as a boy and taught me to behave like one."

She gave a sigh.

"It's going to be hard work becoming a girl after so many years."

"Of course it is, my Lady, and we'll help you in every way we can. Now don't you worry, things'll work out for the best. I'll warn them all in the house and in the stables not to be surprised at your new appearance."

"That is imperative," Georgina emphasised. "I will not want his new Lordship to think we are deceiving him or even putting on an act for his benefit."

"You leave it all to me, my Lady, just as you told me when you was little to look after your pony."

"Did I ask you to do that, Dawson. I suppose that was when I went away with Papa to stay with friends."

"It didn't happen often," Dawson admitted, "but I always knew you trusted me then and I hopes you still trust me now."

"Of course I do," Georgina replied. "It's absolutely essential for the whole family that, when his Lordship does arrive, that he should feel relaxed and at home."

She did not need to say anything more as Dawson understood exactly all that she was asking. He knew, she thought, as much about her family as she did.

*

The next day, obeying her aunt, she rode over to the farms and each farmer and his wife were astonished to see her riding side-saddle and wearing a very becoming riding habit. And she also wore her hat over her wig.

At two of the farms they did not recognise her until she introduced herself.

They were, however, pleased and rather flattered that she had taken the trouble so soon after her father's death to call on them and explain who was taking his place.

As none of them had ever seen Alister, she had to tell them that he had been living abroad for some time.

Now they would have to help him to realise and appreciate what a really magnificent estate he now owned and how well it was worked by those who cared for it.

Finally she went to visit some of the wives in the villages and she made a special effort to talk to the owners of the village shops.

There were not many, but they were vital to those living on the estate and she praised the proprietors and

53

made herself so pleasant that she knew they would talk about her and repeat what she had said to them after she had gone.

Finally she returned to The Castle.

"You didn't 'ave no problem, my Lady?" the Head Groom asked when she dismounted.

"No, I enjoyed my ride, Carter. At the same time I feel that I have much to learn as I have never ridden side-saddle before."

She spoke without thinking and then she glanced over her shoulder before she added,

"But, of course, it would be a big mistake to let the new Earl know that. I trust you all not to mention to him that in the past I have always ridden astride."

"You can trust us not to make trouble, my Lady," Carter assured her with a grin.

Georgina thanked him.

When she went back to The Castle, it seemed very large and empty.

She knew that she was missing her father more than she could express in words or even acknowledge herself.

He had been such an interesting man and she had an empty feeling in her heart that she would never find another man like him.

How could she when he had lived such a full and interesting life, apparently content to ride about the estate with his small daughter.

He had always talked to her as if she was one of his contemporaries.

'There will never be another man like him in my life,' she told herself sadly.

Her father had always disliked tears and he had taught her the way to control herself.

"You may want to cry," he said, "but no real lady cries in public. It's a tiresome and rather ugly expression of your feelings that you should put into words."

Georgina had challenged this by saying that there were few words to express what one felt before one cried and that started a lengthy debate, which they both enjoyed and neither of them came out as the winner. It was the way they passed most evenings together and they talked rather than played games.

Now Georgina felt that she had learnt so much from him without realising that she was actually doing so.

"I miss him so much," she said to the empty room.

Finally she went to the music room where they had held parties when she was a child, but, because they bored her father, there had not been any since her mother's death.

However, her father had been rather musical and he not only played the piano himself but encouraged Georgina to do the same.

Now she sat down in the large empty room and then, opening the piano, she ran her fingers over the keys.

She could remember all too clearly the music that her father had loved which he had played continually.

One was a song that she had learnt to sing when she was quite young and he had often made her sing it to him while he played.

She tried to sing it now, but the tears came into her eyes and her father would have disapproved.

She therefore stood up, shut the piano lid down and walked to the window.

Then she was fighting against the tears that she had not shed at the funeral and had stopped herself from doing even when she was alone.

She gazed out into the garden where the sun was sinking behind the trees.

There were flowers giving a huge splash of colour against the green of the grass and she could hear the rooks going to their nests.

'How could I go away and leave all this?' she asked herself.

She recognised then that she was afraid that Alister would have no use for her and would ask her to leave as soon as possible.

It was with a supreme effort that she prevented herself from crying out and also from praying to her father, wherever he might be at this moment, to save her.

"How could you leave me," Papa?" she asked. "If I am sent away, I will not only be without you but without my home."

It was with the greatest difficulty that she checked the tears from rolling down her cheeks.

Then she walked back upstairs to her room feeling as if she was lost and had nothing left in the world now that she was utterly alone.

*

The following day, however, the sun was shining.

Once she was mounted on a horse, even though it was side-saddle, it was better than sitting moping in The Castle and missing her father every time she drew breath.

She rode for a long time without stopping to see the men who were working or going to a farm or village.

She kept thinking that perhaps this was the last time she would feel that the land was hers and The Castle in the distance was hers too.

'Why, oh why,' she asked herself a hundred times, 'was I not born a boy?'

In which case she would now be the Earl and would be able to do everything the family required of her.

'It's not fair, it's not fair,' she wanted to scream and yet she knew that the laws of succession were not only unfair but highly effective.

Finally she went home.

Although Dawson told her that tea was ready in the drawing room, she first went upstairs to change.

Alister might arrive at any moment or it might be weeks before he turned up.

After all, if they found him in Japan, it was a long journey back over the sea and there was always a chance that he would go first to see one of the family in London before he came to the country.

Equally she knew that she had to be prepared.

She therefore put on another pretty afternoon dress and arranged the wig over her own curly fair hair.

When she looked at herself in the mirror, she found it not only difficult to realise who she was, but also she had to admit that she was quite as good-looking as any of the pictures of her relatives that hung in the picture gallery.

On her instructions the servants had opened all the rooms and indeed many of them had been closed up for a long time. They had dusted all the bedrooms and made them as attractive as possible.

'Just supposing,' she said to herself, 'Alister arrives with a number of friends.'

It would have been very embarrassing to find the beds were not made, the curtains drawn and there was a smell of dust.

She also knew without giving orders that there was plenty of food in the kitchen, not only for the new Earl but for anyone he wished to entertain.

She was aware without being told that the staff had often regretted that there were no evening parties and no big luncheons to cater for.

Although she and her father had always been very appreciative of what came to the table, she knew that just having two people was very different from when there had been the large parties. Her father had given plenty of those when he first inherited the title at which her mother shone as a beautiful and gracious hostess.

Georgina ate her tea alone in the drawing room and looked gratefully at the flowers that had been brought in that day to decorate the room.

When the sun began to sink in the sky, she thought that she should go upstairs to change for dinner.

She had worn a different gown every night even though she had dined alone, thinking that she should see which ones became her and which were likely to impress Alister when he did arrive.

As she picked up the book she had been reading from the sofa and thought that she would take it upstairs, she heard the sound of wheels outside.

She knew only too well that the wheels belonged to a heavy carriage and there was the sound of hooves that told her it was drawn by four horses.

It was then in a sudden panic she wanted to run away.

She was almost sure that, as it was now too late for anyone to call at The Castle, it must be Alister arriving and she was really apprehensive about meeting him.

Then she told herself that, as her father's daughter, she should not be afraid of anything, least of all the man who was to take her beloved father's place.

She stood with her back to the fireplace fighting for breath, telling herself that it was childish and stupid of her to be afraid.

There was the sound of voices in the hall.

Then the door of the drawing room slowly opened and Dawson announced,

"The Earl of Langfield, my Lady."

Georgina felt as if a cold hand was clutching at her throat.

As a man then came into the room, it was with the greatest difficulty that she forced herself to look at him.

He was tall – taller than she expected.

As he walked towards her, she realised that he was far better looking than she had thought he would be.

With a tremendous effort she forced herself to say,

"Welcome to The Castle. As I expect you know, I am your cousin, Georgina."

"As I have been away from England for so long," Alister replied, "I was wondering as I came here if there would be anyone to welcome me. Then I recalled being told that you had always lived here with your father and I am delighted not to find The Castle completely empty."

He spoke in a low voice and, as she shook his hand, she knew instinctively that he was a strong determined man who would not be influenced by anything or anyone.

"I am sure a great number of the family would have been pleased to have been here to greet you," she said, "but no one knew when you would be arriving."

"I was unsure myself just how long the ship would take," Alister answered. "Actually it was quicker than I expected."

"You have come from Japan?" she asked. "It's a country I would love to visit."

"I have enjoyed myself there, but, now I have come home, I expect I will have to live a very different life. I hope that there will be someone to tell me all about it."

"My father liked being alone with me," Georgina answered. "Therefore I am afraid that I am the only person who can answer completely all the questions you will feel obliged to ask. I think I am right in saying that you came here last as a boy."

"I came here last when I was at University just for a luncheon with your father. But I stayed here I think when I was ten or eleven. I much enjoyed riding his horses."

"The stables are still full," Georgina told him and she managed, as she spoke, to force a smile to her lips.

"I expected that," Alister replied. "I was told over and over again how much your father loved his horses and indeed what magnificent ones he had. I only hope when I see them that I will not be disappointed."

"I will be very surprised if you are!" she exclaimed. "But I am sure after a long journey you require a drink."

Even as she spoke, the door opened and Dawson came in with a bottle of champagne in a gold ice-bucket and he was followed by a footman carrying two glasses on a tray.

Another footman had two plates of *petits fours* and sandwiches and he put them down on a table in front of the sofa.

Dawson poured out two glasses of champagne and, as he was about to leave, Georgina said,

"His Lordship is, of course, in the Master suite. As he has come from a warm climate, I am wondering if he would like a fire."

"Certainly not!" Alister intervened at once. "The temperature is perfect as far as I am concerned and a fire would doubtless make me too hot."

"It was very cold last winter," Georgina told him. "And I can assure you that we were very grateful to have fires, especially in the bigger rooms, but nothing seemed to make them really warm."

She was talking just because she felt she had to do so and, when the servants left the room, she said,

"I think I must explain to you that Dawson has been here for years. In fact he came first as a bootboy to my grandfather and gradually rose to become a much trusted and exceptionally outstanding butler."

"That is exactly what I would have expected at The Castle and I imagine that you are staying here to introduce me not only to the staff but to the people on the estate."

Georgina drew in her breath.

"Actually I am staying here as I have nowhere else to go," she replied. "I was hoping, as you are not married, that I could be of real use to you."

Alister looked at her in surprise.

"I learnt years ago that you are your father's only child, but I thought by this time you would be married and I would be alone in The Castle."

"I have been too happy with Papa to think about marriage," Georgina answered, "although actually no one has asked me to be his wife."

"I am surprised at that."

"I have been so very happy with Papa and I helped him with the estate. I thought until you found your feet that you would want me to introduce you to our people and tell you about them."

"I am delighted that you should think of doing so. At the same time I find it extraordinary that you have not been married off, as I was."

There was an unexpectedly hard and bitter note in his voice.

Georgina then remembered how pressure had been brought on him when he was young to marry the woman he had finally hated – a woman who had eventually made him run away to a distant part of the world.

"I expect," she assured him, "that you will find a number of people only too willing to help you. But in the meantime, as I am the one person who really understands the estate and those living on it, I should be delighted to do anything I can to make you appreciate how successful my father has been."

She paused for a moment and, as he did not speak, she went on,

"Despite the war and the recession that followed it, we have managed to keep our heads high."

"I am quite certain that your father was respected and extremely efficient," Alister commented.

"Yes, he was and I am sure you will be impressed by the many new ideas he had for the farms and, of course, his horses are unique."

"I felt sure you would say that, but first, Cousin Georgina, I will want to explore The Castle and I can say in all truth that it is very exciting, in fact thrilling, for me to own anything so large and so important as a castle that has been in the family for so many centuries."

He gave a little laugh before he added,

"I never in my wildest dreams thought I should be the eleventh Earl of Langfield."

"It must have been a surprise," Georgina agreed. "Because when you left England there were several people who were closer relatives to Papa than you were."

"What happened to them?" Alister enquired.

"One died of his war wounds after suffering quite a lot, I understand. Another was drowned in an accident at sea when he was travelling to America and the third was killed in a duel in France, where he returned after the war was over because he had fallen in love."

"That at least was romantic," Alister replied. "But, of course, you will understand that it never occurred to me that I might step into your father's shoes. I can only hope that, having done so, I will not make a mess of it."

He smiled as if he thought it most unlikely.

Georgina could only murmur,

"I am sure you will not do that."

As he sipped his glass, Georgina suggested,

"I am sure after such a long journey you would like a bath. I expect by this time they will have unpacked some of your clothes. Therefore shall I take you upstairs to the Master suite."

Alister rose to his feet.

"Is this castle really mine?" he asked as if he was talking to himself. "I find it hard to believe that I have inherited anything quite so majestic."

"But you have and, as I expect you already know, it is a great responsibility."

Alister looked at her sharply.

"What do you mean by that?" he asked.

"You are Head of the Family and they all depend on you."

"In what way?" he asked.

She thought that she had jumped in at the deep end too quickly and suggested,

"Shall I tell you about it after dinner? I am sure that now you are tired from the journey."

"I think you are prevaricating. Not only in the way you are thinking of me but from the way you have spoken, I am certain that what you have to tell me is of tremendous importance."

He was being cleverer than she expected him to be and, because she was nervous that she might say the wrong thing, she replied,

"It may take quite a time for you to understand all I have to tell you. Therefore as a special dinner is now being prepared for you and our cook, who is the butler's wife, has been practising for days so that everything will please you, I think we should leave the more serious discussions until after dinner."

"Very well," Alister agreed. "But I think you must be aware that you are frightening me. You are also making me very curious. I am wondering if it is all happening just by chance or whether you have thought it out in a rather unexpected and intriguing way."

Georgina laughed.

"Now you are frightening *me*. If we don't want to be late for dinner, I propose that we go upstairs now."

"Very well. But I am sure, because you know what you have to say is so vital, you are distinctly keeping me on a string which is something I very much dislike."

Too late Georgina realised she had taken a wrong step and she should not have mentioned it in the first place.

Because she was worried that she could not carry out the instructions of the family, as they expected her to do, she said quickly,

"Please don't think that I have any other reason for asking you to wait than the fact that my father was always very punctual. As a result dinner will be ready at exactly eight o'clock."

"Then, of course, I must wait to hear what you have to tell me," Alister replied. "Naturally I am anxious to see the Master suite which will undoubtedly make me feel very proud of myself."

"You will find it very impressive. Remember that your ancestors have slept there for over six centuries."

"I only hope they will not haunt me! In fact they may sit around when I want to go to sleep, telling me that I am incompetent and feeling ashamed that they have been succeeded by someone who does not live up to their high standards!"

Georgina smiled.

"Some of them have very strange standards as you will find if you read the history of the family. But it would be very difficult to find fault with either my father or my grandfather."

"Then I must follow them as best I can."

There was undoubtedly a twist to his lips and a touch of sarcasm in the way he spoke that made Georgina feel uneasy.

Because she felt it was a mistake to go on talking, she walked towards the door and Alister reached it before she did to open it for her.

They walked in silence across the hall where there were four footmen on duty.

Again in silence they walked up the magnificent staircase that led to the first floor.

Georgina wondered if she should point out to him the flags by the Mediaeval fireplace that had been brought back by their ancestors from battles over the centuries.

She felt that that sort of lesson would last until tomorrow and for the moment she should keep to small talk of what was currently happening and make it as easy as possible.

She was aware, however, that Alister was looking round him as they went along the first floor corridor where all the State bedrooms were situated.

On each door was printed the name of the bedroom and most of them were called after the King, Queen or Royal personage who had slept in them in the past.

At the far end the Master suite consisted of a very large and impressive bedroom, a boudoir and a dressing room with a number of wardrobes for his clothes.

The bed which had been handed down the centuries was an enormous four-poster with carved pillars of birds and wild game.

There were heavy curtains of deep red velvet and the headboard over the bed displayed the family Coat of Arms picked out in gold and mother-of-pearl.

Alister did not speak, but stood for a while looking at the bed which had a gold candelabrum on each side of it.

Then unexpectedly he laughed.

"I will certainly feel grand, in fact Royal, in such a magnificent and imposing bed!"

"My father always said it was as comfortable as it appeared," Georgina answered. "If you have not brought a valet with you, I know that Dawson will look after you."

As she spoke, Dawson came in from the dressing room followed by a footman.

"We've unpacked everythin' that we thought you'd require, my Lord," he explained. "The rest will, of course, be done tomorrow."

"I am very grateful, thank you," Alister replied.

As he spoke, Georgina moved towards the door.

"I will be downstairs in the drawing room," she told him, "just before eight o'clock, so there is no need for you to rush."

She did not wait to hear his reply, but hurried into the passage and almost ran towards her own room.

It was only when she had shut herself in that she felt she could breathe freely.

She had somehow thought that Alister would find everything rather awe-inspiring and she was sure that it would be hard for him to find his feet in a completely strange environment to anything he had found abroad.

Alister was, she guessed, not particularly awestruck by The Castle and she had the feeling that he was intending to make it quite clear that he had no use for her.

It was not what he had said, but the way she had felt his reaction to everything she had told him.

Although he had said that he was surprised and overcome with The Castle, it had not been entirely true.

He was clearly too much aware of his own personal appearance to be awed and he was certainly not intimidated by his ancestors.

'I am quite certain of one thing,' Georgina mused as she walked to the window, 'he will not do anything he does not want to do. If Aunt Marjory thinks I can twist him round my little finger, she is very much mistaken.'

CHAPTER FOUR

Mrs. Dawson had excelled herself with the dinner and Georgina knew that she must have been thinking it out for days before Alister arrived.

Every course was a delight, not only to the tongue but to the eye.

However, she realised that he was not particularly impressed, but at the same time he was enjoying his food.

She asked him to tell her about the countries he had visited. He did so, but in an off-hand way as if he thought that she would not be interested in any detail.

But because Georgina realised only too well that she must be quiet, gentle and appreciative of everything he did, good or bad, she talked in a low feminine voice.

Although her questions to him were intelligent, she was careful to make it appear that she was a pupil at the foot of a Master.

When the last course was finished, Georgina said,

"We usually have coffee in the drawing room or wherever we are sitting, but perhaps you would prefer to have it in here."

"The drawing room will indeed suit me as well as anywhere else," Alister replied.

"In which case you will not wish me to leave you to your port," Georgina answered, "and perhaps you would like to tell Dawson if you prefer a liqueur."

"I want neither," Alister retorted almost sharply.

Georgina realised that she had made a mistake and she should have left it to him as Master of The Castle to decide what he drank, but she thought on the first night it would be advisable to tell him what had been her father's habits.

However, she rose with dignity from the table and walked unhurriedly towards the door.

Dawson, waiting to hear what was required, turned to open it for her.

As she walked past him, she said,

"Thank you, Dawson, and do tell Mrs. Dawson that it was a most delicious dinner. I enjoyed every mouthful."

Dawson smiled and she then walked on wondering if Alister would also say something complimentary.

But she did not hear him say anything.

When he joined her ten minutes later in the drawing room, she knew that it would be tactless to ask him any more questions.

She sat down on what had been her usual place on the sofa and Alister took one of the armchairs.

There was a long silence until Dawson brought in the coffee with one of the footmen carrying the tray and he then offered Alister one of the liqueurs carried by another footman.

When the servants had left and she was sipping her coffee, Alister declared,

"Now I suppose you are waiting to tell me what I would much rather hear from the secretary or one of the managers of the estate."

Georgina looked at him in surprise and then she replied quickly,

"Oh, no! I am not going to tell you anything about the estate until you ask me directly to do so. Of course the manager will be waiting to meet you and as you can well imagine he will be somewhat long-winded about it."

She thought he might laugh, but instead he asked,

"So what do you wish to tell me?"

Georgina drew in her breath.

"It's about the family," she answered.

"The family!" he exclaimed in surprise. "And what have they to do with it."

"They are afraid that you will not know, as you have been abroad so long, that in your new position as Earl and owner of The Castle, all the family, including myself, rely entirely on you."

Alister stared at her.

"I don't understand what you are saying."

"It has always been the habit in this family, as in others that are very old, that we keep to the rules which existed when The Castle was first built. They are that the Head of the Family is responsible for every member of it."

"In what way?" he enquired. "I don't follow you."

"Perhaps I am putting it badly," she replied. "It is that the Earl of Langfield, whoever he might be, supplies every one of the family with money that he holds on their behalf. They are all, in fact, entirely dependent on him."

Alister sat up in his chair a little further.

Then he quizzed,

"Is this completely true?"

"Of course it is! I thought, as you are a member of the family, you would have been aware of the custom."

"I had no idea of it," he confessed. "As a matter of fact my mother left me money when she died and before that gave me a large allowance and so did my father. I have never had to worry about money in any way."

"That is very pleasant for you," Georgina remarked. "But the rest of the family rely entirely on the goodwill and the generosity of the Head of it."

There was silence for a moment and then Alister said as if he could hardly believe that what she was saying was correct,

"Are you telling me that I have to dole out to our relations the money they wish to spend otherwise they will have none?"

"Some of them have money from the woman or the man they married," Georgina told him. "But the majority, including my aunt, who is Papa's sister, have always had a large allowance from him. They would be almost destitute without it."

"This is the most extraordinary arrangement I have ever heard," Alister exclaimed sharply.

"It happened at one time in most of the old families in England," Georgina replied. "But I think some of them have broken away now and prefer to be independent."

She paused before she went on,

"Equally those who have not done so would be utterly impoverished if they had not been looked after."

Alister rose to stand in front of the fireplace.

"It never occurred to me," he sighed after a long pause, "that I would have to be Father Christmas to the family who I am not particularly interested in!"

Georgina drew in her breath and then she said as quietly as she could,

"I am afraid that if you don't look after them they will be very unhappy and some will be poverty stricken."

"But surely, if they have had money all their lives, where has it come from?"

"It has come from the reigning Earl."

"It's the most ridiculous idea I have ever heard of," Alister said angrily. "Supposing he dislikes someone in the family or quarrels with him, do you mean he can cut them off without a penny?"

"It would be very cruel and unkind if he did, but it is possible," Georgina affirmed.

"It's also out of date and extremely dangerous!"

"Why should you say that?" Georgina asked.

She forgot for a moment to make herself soft, sweet and gentle as she had managed to do all through dinner.

Now without thinking she remarked,

"It may seem absurd to you, but, as it has worked perfectly well for hundreds of years, you can hardly expect a family as ancient and respected as ours not to keep the old traditions going."

"How can you be sure?" Alister asked. "Many of the family might have been cut off without a penny and died in complete poverty."

"If they had, there is no mention of it in the history books," Georgina informed him. "Nor do I think any man who calls himself a gentleman would behave in such a way to those who are totally dependent on him."

Alister turned and walked away towards one of the windows and, pulling back the ornate curtains, he opened the window and gazed out.

The moon had risen and the garden was flooded with a silver light that was very beautiful.

He stood gazing out without speaking for a while.

Then he turned and walked back to stand as he had before in front of the fireplace.

"Is that all you have to tell me?" he asked.

"There are many other things I could tell you," she replied. "But I think that this is the most important and, of course, you will understand that a number of our relations have been waiting anxiously for your return."

"I am not surprised," Alister agreed, "and so the sooner I make them independent the better."

"Independent?" Georgina queried.

"I suppose I could give them some money outright so that they need not come troubling me again and need no longer watch to see if I am generous or not."

"But of course you must not do anything like that!" Georgina cried. "It would upset everyone! The whole family has been quite content to accept that the reigning Earl should look after them and that they can turn to him with their troubles and difficulties and he would do his best to solve them."

She paused and when he did not speak she went on,

"It is a most important position and, as my father always said, they looked on him as the Father of the Clan and he must behave as a father should to his children."

"It was all very well for your father to talk like that," Alister replied. "He had lived here all his life and been close, I suppose, to every one of his relations who, as you say, depended on him. I have been abroad and don't even know the names of half of my relatives and actually have no wish to know any of them."

"You must not say that," Georgina protested. "Can you not understand that this is a wonderful position for anyone to have?"

She threw out her hands as she continued,

"You own this castle. You own nearly half the County and you are looked up to and respected, not only by the family but by everyone in the vicinity."

"I can assure you here and now, that it is something I don't want. I want to lead my own life. I want to enjoy myself as I have managed to do these past years because I have been on my own. And most of all I have no wish to have relatives, whoever they may be, screaming at me for help all the time!"

It was with the greatest difficulty that Georgina bit back the words that came to her lips.

She was absolutely horrified at the idea that Alister was not pleased at taking on such a distinguished position.

If he was not grateful for it, then he should at least be grateful for the possessions and the large sum of money that was now at his disposal.

It was only by using every ounce of her willpower that she prevented herself from replying to him angrily, telling him that he was being outrageously selfish apart from anything else.

Almost as if her father was guiding her and helping her, she knew that if she quarrelled with him he would throw her out and perhaps never speak to her again.

Twisting her fingers so that they hurt, she managed to say in a very quiet voice,

"What you have just said is, I find, very upsetting."

"Why should it worry you particularly?" he asked sharply.

"Because I am not only totally dependent on you," she replied, "but this is my home. I have been here – since I was born and have – nowhere else to go."

The words came jerkily from between her lips and Alister stared at her.

"Is this true?"

"Absolutely true," Georgina replied. "If you send me away, I have no idea where I will go."

"You have plenty of relatives," Alister retorted.

"I have seen very little of them during the years and they will have no wish for me to be with them, especially if you don't provide them with any money."

"I have not said I will not provide for them," Alister answered. "I only think it is a ridiculously absurd idea that I should become, as you say, a father to these people who I don't know and for whom I dislike being responsible."

"I have been brought up to believe that blood is important and that one has an affinity to those who belong to the same Family Tree, who like ourselves believe that they must obey and admire the man who represents the whole family to the world."

Alister walked across the room and back again before he replied,

"I understand what you are saying. At the same time I think it is a lot of nonsense. What would happen if I paid off the relatives and had little more to do with them."

Georgina was silent for a moment as she thought it out and then she replied,

"To begin with they would be very upset, although they might well appreciate the money that you would give them. But you must understand that Papa invested it very carefully. Here on the estate we make enough every year to keep it all going. Also we provide for our pensioners, those who are sick and the families who suffered terribly from the war when the father and sons were killed."

As she finished speaking, she realised that Alister had been listening to her attentively.

He had obviously no idea that this was expected of him.

"It may be difficult for you," Georgina went on, "to understand exactly what I am saying. But if you had been at Papa's funeral which, as he had died so suddenly, was attended by very few of the family but by almost everyone on the estate, you would have known what he meant to them and how unhappy they were at losing him."

She was thinking as she spoke how the women had cried and how the men had appeared tight-lipped and pale when they carried his coffin.

They were upset not just because he had employed them but because ever since they had been born the Earl of The Castle had been of great consequence in their lives.

They had felt, although perhaps they did not put it into words, that they belonged to him.

She wondered now what she should do and how she could appeal to Alister.

Then, as if she had been guided, she said,

"I know that this has been a shock to you. But I suggest, instead of making up your mind now, you allow me to ride round the estate with you tomorrow when you will meet the people and see for yourself what they feel about you and forget the relatives for the moment."

Unexpectedly Alister smiled.

"Now I think you are being reasonable so as to make me see that I really have no chance of escaping from this unwelcome and quite horrifying burden."

"If you feel like that, I am quite sure you will find some way of preventing yourself from being involved," Georgina told him.

"How can I do that?" Alister enquired.

"For the moment I don't know the answer, but I imagine that there is one. Perhaps you could give your responsibilities to a man who is trained for such a position. Then you could go back to the other side of the world where you have just come from."

"Are you telling me if I did so that I could forget you all?" Alister enquired.

"You could try to do so, but, if you ask me to tell you the truth, I don't think you would succeed."

She felt as if the words were put into her mouth.

Once again Alister walked to the open window and he stood there without moving.

But she had an idea that the moon was talking to him.

He was also moved, although he did not wish to be, with the beauty of the gardens and the stars coming out over the tops of the trees.

It was a vista that had always appealed to her until she felt that the moonlight and the stars were moving from the Heavens into herself – or perhaps she was even moving towards them.

Yet always the beauty of it swept away anything that was trivial and unimportant.

Georgina had always gone to her bed thinking only how happy she was and how much she loved her home and her father.

Alister stood at the window without moving.

Then again, as if she was being told exactly what to do, Georgina rose very quietly from the sofa where she had been sitting and slipped out of the room.

She did not speak and was quite certain that Alister did not hear her go.

As she ran up the stairs to her room, she thought that the moonlight and the stars would tell him better than she had done where his duty lay.

What was more, he would find it difficult to forget not only the beauty that lay in front of him but The Castle he was seeing it from.

All the Langfields who had lived there had left an impression in The Castle that was impossible to ignore and Georgina had been aware of ever since she had been born.

She knew now that if she did have to leave The Castle she would leave something of herself behind, just as those who had lived there for centuries had, each of them, left something when they passed on to another world.

'It is The Castle who will tell him what he must do,' she reflected. 'He will know if he stays here for long enough that it is impossible not to listen to what it says.'

When she finally climbed into bed and blew out the candles, she was desperately afraid in case she had failed to convince Alister that he had a very vital part to play in the future and however much he tried he could not slip away from it.

*

It was early in the morning when Georgina awoke and she found that, despite going to bed feeling worried and anxious, she had slept dreamlessly.

The sun was shining although it was not yet high in the Heavens and she could hear the birds singing in the garden.

She jumped out of bed and, because she was in a hurry, she found it difficult to remember that she must put on her female riding dress rather than her breeches and she must wear a soft cotton blouse instead of a shirt.

There was no need for her to wear anything round her neck and a hat was really unnecessary.

Then she remembered that last night she had been wearing her wig and without it she would certainly look strange.

So she put on a cap that she had sometimes worn when she was racing or steeplechasing. At least it hid the majority of her curls and the fact that there were practically none at the back of her head.

Then she ran down the stairs and, going out of The Castle, she reached the stables without seeing anyone.

A sleepy young groom who was in charge touched his forelock when she appeared and, without being told, he hurried to put a bridle on one of the horses she loved better than all the rest.

It was one her father had given her two years ago for her birthday and she found that Sunlight was one of the finest and fastest horses she had ever ridden.

Thanking the young groom for his help, she rode out of the back of the stables onto the flat land that led to her father's Racecourse.

He had erected it originally as an amusement for himself and his daughter and what had been a small race meeting to entertain themselves and those who worked on the estate had grown into a very much larger one.

Because he had such excellent horses and they were well known for their brilliance on other Racecourses, it had soon become a yearly event.

For one day of the year at least The Castle was full with the owners of racehorses and their wives who came to see them win, also a number of the family who felt it polite if nothing else to appear at Langfield Castle on the day when it was at its most popular.

At first her father had not allowed Georgina to take part in the races because she had been too young and later it was because professional jockeys rode and he thought that she should not become associated with them.

Then, as she had pleaded with him, she had finally been allowed to ride his horses and then, because she was dressed as a boy, few onlookers, unless they were members of the family, had the slightest idea that she was a girl.

Now, as she took her horse round the Racecourse, she was thinking what excitement there had been the first time she had won a race.

After that her father was quite upset if she was not the winner of at least two or three races at each meeting.

She was just taking one of the most difficult jumps in style when she realised that she was not alone on the Racecourse.

She had for the moment forgotten about Alister and all the difficulties he was causing. She was thinking only of how well her horse jumped and how pleased her father would have been with her.

As Alister came to join her, he began,

"I remember hearing about this Racecourse before I left England. I did not think then I would have a chance of riding on it."

Georgina smiled at him.

"As you are doing so now, I will race you round it and I can assure you that you will have every chance of winning on that particular mount."

"I was told his name is Firefly," Alister said, "and I think it's an appropriate name for him."

"I am certain that if you speak to him positively," Georgina replied, "he will realise that you are a guest at the moment. Therefore he will not be so afraid as he might be if he learnt that you are his owner!"

Alister's eyes twinkled.

"Now I know that you are using another handcuff on me very discreetly so that I cannot escape."

"When you have ridden Firefly, I don't think you will want to escape," Georgina assured him. "Shall we start from here?"

Alister pulled Firefly into place alongside her and, as she obviously expected him to start the race, he called out,

"One, two three, *go!*"

They both started off at the same moment and both horses took the first and second jumps in style and Alister realised that his mount was outstanding.

It was a delight he had not experienced while he had been abroad.

When they came to the finishing post, Georgina, although she had never done it before, deliberately pulled in Sunlight so that Alister won the race by a length.

"You have won and I salute you," she laughed as she trotted up to him.

"I am very pleased with myself," Alister responded. "Equally I have a suspicion, although I am reticent to put it into words, that Sunlight could have overtaken me."

"You must never argue when the credit is yours," Georgina answered coyly.

"Then I merely thank you for a delightful race. I must ask you to tell me how often the races which your father initiated take place here and when is the next one to be expected?"

"In two months' time," Georgina informed him. "If you don't win every race as Papa was capable of doing, everyone in the stables will be disappointed."

Alister chuckled.

"What about the other contenders?"

"To excuse themselves they say that they would not like to upset his Lordship by preventing him from winning so many races."

Alister chuckled again.

"Are you expecting to say the same of me?"

"But of course. When I saw you riding just now for the first time, I should have known that you were one of the family even if we had not been introduced!"

Alister thought this amusing.

"Now that is a real compliment," he said. "I am sure that it is something I must always cherish."

They rode on and Georgina showed him the wood nearest the house, which she had loved ever since she had been a child.

Without thinking about it, she told him how she had always believed that there were goblins under the trees and that fairies lived along the edge of the stream which ran through that part of the wood.

Then to her surprise Alister remarked,

"Just as you believe there are fairies in the garden."

"How did you know that?" Georgina asked him.

"I am sure, as you live here, that is what you were bound to feel," he answered. "I suppose many years ago when I was a little boy I too believed in fairies."

"Whether you believe in them or not, you will find them here and I have always thought, although I may be wrong, that they have also invaded The Castle itself!"

She spoke seriously as she would have done to her father and she was suddenly aware that she was talking to Alister, who had been very different last night.

She had almost hated him because she thought that he was going to upset everything that was important to the family and that he would not care for The Castle and the estate as she did.

But now, seeing him riding on a horse, she was impressed even though she had not intended to be.

He was indeed an excellent rider and again, as if he realised what she was thinking, he said,

"I have ridden a great deal while I have been away exploring. Not, of course, horses like this, but very strange ones. Some of them were very weird and had odd ways of ridding themselves of a rider that could be very painful!"

Georgina giggled.

"I thought you were going to tell me that you had ridden nearly every sort of animal besides a horse!"

"It's true," Alister replied. "I did have a favourite elephant and a very un-favourite mule!"

"Did it unseat you?"

"It had a terrible habit of turning round and biting my legs, while my elephant was slow but trustworthy."

"You know I am longing to hear all about your travels," Georgina remarked. "But I have been too polite to press you into talking about them until you wished to."

"I don't think you would be particularly interested," Alister told her, "as they were sometimes long distances and a great amount of discomfort, which all women would find distasteful."

"Except me," she said. "I think, when everything goes too smoothly, it's boring. It is always the unexpected and perhaps the most uncomfortable moments of a journey or a ride that one remembers afterwards and laughs about."

Alister turned to look at her before he asked,

"Is that the truth? I have never met a woman yet who did not make a fuss over everything that went wrong on a journey and complained forcibly if not tearfully at being uncomfortable."

"Perhaps you have been unlucky. You know as well as I do that if everything in our lives moved smoothly and without any ups and downs, we would soon be bored. It is the downs that bring out the best in us."

"In men but not women," Alister parried.

"Then you must have been unlucky," Georgina said again.

She did not say any more and, as they trotted out of the wood, she allowed Sunlight to gallop ahead and for the moment any further conversation was impossible.

As she turned towards The Castle, as it was almost time for breakfast, she thought however much he might fight against it, undoubtedly Alister's blood was pulsating in the right places.

Sooner or later it would guide him into the right way for a Langfield to behave.

Breakfast was waiting for them, as Georgina had expected, when they reached The Castle.

Dawson told the new Earl that there was a manager and a number of other men who ran the estate waiting to see him.

When they then went into the dining room and the servants had withdrawn, Alister enquired,

"What is all this about? Why are there a number of men waiting to talk to me?"

"They want to meet you and they want to show you how brilliantly they have worked to make the estate known and admired all over this part of England."

"Is that true?" Alister asked her. "Or are you just saying it for effect."

"I never tell a lie if I can help it. Papa always inferred that lies are only spoken by thieves and cowards."

Alister laughed.

"I am sure your father was right. At the same time people boast because they want to seem important. I want to learn the truth about the estate now that it is mine."

"You don't have to be told that the Racecourse is a good one," Georgina smiled.

"No, that's true!" Alister replied. "I realised, just as soon as I saw it, that it is well laid out and the jumps are fantastic."

"Papa expected perfection in everything," Georgina told him, "not just for his own satisfaction but because The

Castle and the estate represented the family to the world. He wanted the Langs to be better than anyone else."

"Of course you are pointing out to me in a very clever way that I am a Lang," Alister declared.

"But of course you are! Even if you had been in parts of the world where the people have never heard of us, you must have known at the back of your mind that you were successful in everything you did because you were one of the family."

"How did you know that I have been successful?" he asked sharply.

"I think if you had not been or if you had been unhappy, you would have come home," Georgina replied. "It is what everyone does when things go wrong. As you stayed away, everything must have been right for you."

Almost despite himself Alister laughed.

"You really do have an amusing way of expressing yourself," he told her. "Of course you are right although I hate to admit it."

"When you are out today and can see what you now own, remember that the men showing it all to you will be waiting anxiously for your praise."

She smiled at him before continuing,

"If you congratulate them on what they have done, they will work for you even harder in the future than they have worked in the past for my father."

"How can you be sure of that?" Alister enquired.

"I am sure because it is human nature and because I know the people here. Whether they admit it or not, they are intensely proud of being employed on this estate."

Alister was listening intently, so she went on,

"They will each be worrying quietly to themselves whether you will be satisfied with them and expect them to carry on, as they have done in the past or make frightening changes that they will not understand."

Then in a very small voice Georgina added,

"What is more frightening still is if you don't need them. Then they will have nowhere to go and nothing to look forward to."

As she finished speaking, there was a silence and then Alister asked,

"Are you thinking at the back of your mind that I might shut up The Castle and go abroad?"

"I had occurred to me," Georgina replied honestly. "Equally I think it very unlikely."

"Why?" he asked abruptly.

"Because overnight you have become the Monarch of all you survey. You are important, in fact as important as a King, because this Kingdom is yours. Every man and woman in it admires and serves you not only because of the money you give to them but because their home, their family and their energy is all yours."

Alister did not speak and, finishing his breakfast, he pushed his chair back from the table and walked, as he had done the night before, to the window.

Now he was looking out at the garden, which was a mass of flowers and the sunshine that was making his new world very beautiful was shining in on him.

On his way home when he knew the tenth Earl was dead, he had disliked the idea of coming back to England, of meeting the relatives he remembered and being bored at the thought of those he had not yet met.

When he had left England, he had hated not only his wife but his father and everyone who had forced him into marrying a woman who had made his life a hell.

She had fought against him with every breath that she drew and every word she spoke. She wanted to be top dog and she wanted to beat him at everything he did.

He found himself not only loathing her but feeling that every English woman was like her in that they wanted to win because they were women.

They wanted to take away from men the strength and authority they had had ever since the world began.

He had found that women were so very different in other countries, especially in the East and he had enjoyed being in Japan more than anywhere else.

Japanese women had pandered to him and flattered him. They had made him feel, as the Englishwomen had failed to do, that he was not only a man but in every way their superior.

Yet now, even though he was fighting against it, for some reason he could not understand he was beginning to feel that this was his world.

Although he still had no wish to admit it, he was King of The Castle.

CHAPTER FIVE

After breakfast they went to the stables and once again Georgina found herself riding Sunlight.

"We will have to be fair and ride the other horses sometimes," she said to Alister. "We don't want them to be jealous if we take Sunlight and Firefly out every time."

He laughed.

"Do you think they really notice?"

"Of course they do. Papa always taught me to talk to my horse and I am sure that he understands every word I say."

Alister laughed again.

He thought that she was quite right and they would have to exercise the other horses and he was certain that the grooms would not do it as well as they did.

They rode over the fields and called at one of the farms. The farmer and his wife were delighted to see the new Earl.

They showed him proudly how well the crops had sold the previous year, also their lambs which were already arriving and they felt that they would have a larger number than in previous years.

Georgina had already told Alister that this was the most successful farm on the estate. He congratulated the farmer warmly and Georgina thought that he had a very good way with the people of the estate.

She had been a little nervous in case he was too haughty or did not speak to them as if he understood what they were doing.

She need not have worried.

He was, she observed, as friendly and as interested as she had hoped he would be.

They rode on to another farm, which was not quite so prosperous and the farmer and his family told Alister they had had a bad crop last year, but hoped for a much better one this year.

He spoke to them encouragingly and she thought he was certainly making himself popular and the word would go from farm to farm and cottage to cottage that he was the right person to take her father's place.

They spent some time riding over the fields and, when they returned for luncheon, Alister asked,

"How much of the estate have we already done?"

"Very little really," Georgina replied. "In fact there are many, many more acres for you to see and at least three very large farms."

"I had no idea I had inherited such an enormous Empire," Alister sighed.

"You will soon get used to it," Georgina promised. "I hope you will understand when I congratulate you on being splendid this morning."

His eyes twinkled as he enquired,

"Did you expect me to be anything else?"

"I was a bit apprehensive that, having lived abroad for so long, you would have forgotten that English people are very proud and take umbrage very quickly if people condescend to them."

"So that is what you thought I might do!" Alister protested.

"I was afraid of it," she answered. "Because I love these people so much, I would not want them to be hurt or in any way have cause to criticise their new owner."

She spoke as if it really mattered to her and Alister thought that in all his long acquaintance with women he had never known anyone who cared so much about the ordinary people working in the fields.

Because he was curious, he could not help asking,

"Does it really matter to you so much, Georgina?"

"Of course it does. I have known everyone round here since I was born. I know how much they respected my father and believed that he cared as much for them as they did for him."

Alister was silent for a moment and then he said,

"When I heard that I had to take your father's place, my first impulse was to refuse to return to England. Then, because I felt it was my duty, I came, but was determined as soon as it was possible to return to the East."

Georgina gave a cry of horror.

"But how could you do that? How could you leave all these people to suffer because you are not here? The family, even if you provide for them, would not feel it was the same as if they could not turn to you in their troubles and ask your advice on anything serious."

"Like what?" Alister asked sharply.

Georgina thought for a moment and then she said,

"They used to come to my father if their children were in trouble. They asked his advice as to which schools and Universities their sons should attend. They relied on him to help them when their daughters were *debutantes*."

"In what way?"

Georgina smiled.

"He usually lent them the house in London so that they could give a large ball. I remember hearing about two balls that were held here and everyone in the County came. Although I was too young to remember them, I was told that they were huge successes."

"What did he do for you?" Alister enquired.

There was silence.

"I am waiting for an answer," he said after a few moments had passed.

"Well, it was rather difficult. Papa was not very keen on taking me to London because there was so much to be done here. Quite frankly I did not want large parties."

She was thinking as she was speaking that that was a reasonable answer to his question.

Of course the real answer was that, as her father had treated her as if she was a boy, there was no reason for her to be presented at Court – or to be a *debutante* as other girls were when they were seventeen.

"So you just stayed here in the country? Surely that was extremely remiss when you should have been meeting young gentlemen who would propose to you. You would then have a chance of having another estate that, of course, would be inherited by your children."

Georgina thought that this was dangerous ground, so she asked,

"Are you going to spend time in London? After all it must be very different now from when you went away."

"No! Definitely not!" he exclaimed. "From what I have seen, I will have plenty to keep me occupied here."

Georgina smiled.

"That is what I hoped you would say. It reminds me that Mr. Benson is coming today and he will give you the accounts of what the estate made last year and – "

She paused for a moment and then she went on almost bravely,

" – also he will tell you how much Papa gave all the relatives who, as I have told you, relied on him."

Alister did not answer and she knew that they were back on delicate ground. She therefore said,

"Now where I am going to take you this afternoon is, I think, particularly interesting. I know that you will be thrilled with the black sheep this farm has concentrated on. They have been a great success locally."

"Why?" Alister enquired.

"You will hardly believe it, but the people believe that a black sheep brings luck to the whole flock."

She smiled at him as she continued,

"It's true that our sheep have done extremely well at the markets. Buyers from other Counties have been coming to us as they want to increase their own flock."

"Do you believe that black sheep bring them luck?"

"I think actually their luck has been in themselves," Georgina replied "because they work hard and believe in their own animals."

She paused for a moment before she added,

"I think even sheep know when they are loved."

"Perhaps you are right," Alister agreed. "When I heard you speaking to Sunlight, I thought that he pricked up his ears and was listening to everything you said."

"Of course he was. Papa gave him to me for my seventeenth birthday. I think that I have loved him more than any other horse I have ever owned."

Alister sat back in his chair.

"So you expect me to love my horses, my sheep and presumably my pigs and anything else that is bred on the estate."

"*Yes*," Georgina replied almost defiantly. "I want you also to love The Castle, its contents and every member of your large and delightful family."

Alister held up his hands.

"You frighten me," he told her. "I don't feel like that towards animals or people and I have no wish to be pushed by you into feeling it."

Georgina was silent. She thought that perhaps she had asked for too much too quickly.

It was he who must tell her what to do, rather than for her to tell him.

She gave a little sigh.

It was difficult after being treated by her father as a man to quickly appreciate that as a woman she should be subservient and let her Lord and Master do all the talking.

The silence between them was broken by Dawson providing them with an excellent cheese that he said came from one of the local farms.

"It's been sent, your Lordship, as a present," he informed him. "I know they'd appreciate it if you'd send them a short letter of thanks."

"I will naturally thank them," Alister replied in a hard voice and Dawson realised that he had pushed too far.

"It's an exceptionally fine cheese, my Lord, and it's just beginning to be known outside the County, so the farmer hopes your Lordship'll like it."

He left the room before Alister could reply.

Because Georgina thought that the atmosphere was somewhat awkward, she ate in silence.

When luncheon was over, they went to the study where Dawson usually served coffee.

"Why do we have it here," Alister asked, "instead of the dining room as is usual?"

"I think it was because Papa was always anxious to go back to his writing desk," Georgina told him. "Or else to read the newspapers which usually arrive about twelve o'clock. In fact you see they are already there arranged on a stool in front of the fireplace."

Alister did not answer. He merely picked up one of the newspapers and opened it out.

Because he obviously did not want to talk to her, Georgina sat on the sofa and sipped her coffee in silence.

Then Alister gave an exclamation.

"What is it?" she asked.

"You would hardly believe it," he replied, "but there is a long article here about your father's death and reporting that I have inherited from him."

"I hope that they have not said too much about the house," Georgina said quickly. "Papa was always afraid that if they mentioned too much about the pictures and the other treasures we have here, it would invite a burglary."

"Very likely I should imagine," Alister answered. "This is certainly written by someone who knows what The Castle contains."

Georgina gave a cry of horror.

"Papa always said that was dangerous. When the newspapers asked him to describe what was in The Castle, he always said there were just pictures of his ancestors and furniture that had been here for years."

"Well, they have given a very concise list of the best pictures in the Gallery," Alister declared. "They have mentioned as well the French furniture that was brought over at the time of the French Revolution."

Georgina sighed.

"In which case we will not only have to be careful of burglars but of people who are sight-seeing who think that everyone who has a castle like this should open it to the public."

"Which it will never be as long as I am alive," Alister said positively. "There are many burglars in every country and the mere idea that we have a large number of classic pictures here would bring them running."

"Oh, don't say that," Georgina begged, "it frightens me! But the doors have special locks on them as you may have noticed and the windows have been provided with shutters that are supposed to be closed every night."

"Supposed?"

Georgina smiled.

"As you can imagine as there are so many windows some always get forgotten and Papa used to go round last thing at night to make sure that they were all closed."

"Are you suggesting that I should do the same?"

"No, of course not. Now you are here we can have more footmen and, of course, a nightwatchman which Papa felt was unnecessary when just he and I were alone and there were no disclosures in the newspapers."

Alister was frowning and Georgina was wondering what she should say.

After a moment's silence Alister said,

"I am going to walk around the house and look for myself to see if it is properly protected."

He did not ask her to go with him and, when he left the room, she picked up the newspaper he had been reading and read it herself.

The article had obviously been written by someone who had visited The Castle and knew the details of a great number of the pictures.

It also described the French furniture and made a special reference to the beauty of the private Chapel and the Master bedroom.

Georgina read it from beginning to end and she wondered who on earth could have made such an enticing story out of The Castle.

Of course the local people had come from time to time, but she could not believe that the Lord Lieutenant or anyone like him would have written in the newspaper.

But, whoever it was, it was someone who actually knew The Castle, someone who was aware that Alister, as the new Earl, had been abroad for years.

'Whoever has done it has made mischief,' Georgina thought. 'Now things might not be quite as easy as they have appeared.'

She was afraid that before Alister had really settled down and had learnt all she wanted him to know about the estate, they might call on him and somehow interfere.

Her suspicions were to prove only too true.

Two days later, when she hoped that Alister had forgotten the newspaper article, they had a visitor.

They were having a late tea, having gone to the furthest Northern part of the estate.

Alister was interested in a herd of milking cows that the farmer had bred for some years. They were indeed fine-looking beasts and the proud owner claimed that they gave more milk than any other cows in the vicinity.

There were also some pretty calves that Georgina found delightful and the farmer had shown them his geese.

It had been a very successful afternoon, Georgina had felt, as they were riding home and Alister had seemed more at ease with her than he had been since he arrived.

Tea was in the study because Alister had ordered it to be sent there rather than to the drawing room.

Georgina was just pouring the tea for both of them when Dawson announced,

"Lady Lawson, my Lord."

Georgina looked up and saw with annoyance one of their neighbours that she had always disliked and her father too had found Lady Lawson almost intolerable.

They had managed to refuse the invitations she sent them and had deliberately not invited her to The Castle.

She was a well-known hostess in London and her husband, Sir Albert, had never been popular in the County.

Her father had described him as 'an intolerable bore and the worst type of Social climber'.

Georgina had thought that his wife was very much the same except that she was noted for running after every young man in the County and there were quite a number of people who considered her both fast and somewhat vulgar.

As she entered the room, Georgina wished that she had been sensible enough to tell Dawson that they were not at home to the Lawsons if they called.

But she had, in fact, forgotten about her.

She had been so busy showing Alister around the estate she had forgotten that he would be of great interest to others in the County.

Distinctly overdressed for the country with heavily mascarared eyes, Lady Lawson then sailed into the room smiling and held out her hand to Alister.

"I have been waiting to welcome you," she cooed, "and I had no idea that you had already arrived until I read about it in the newspaper."

Alister murmured something non-committal under his breath and Lady Lawson rambled on,

"It's so wonderful you are here. You must allow me to introduce you to so many other people in the County who will be thrilled to meet you. In fact my husband and I want to give a dinner party for you on Wednesday night – or perhaps you would prefer it to be at the weekend when, of course, more people will be arriving from London."

"I am afraid," Alister replied, "that, as I have just arrived, I am very busy. Although it is very kind of you to invite me, you can understand I am still finding my feet. There is so much to do here I hardly have time to breathe."

He spoke so sincerely that Georgina thought he was being very clever, but at the same time she wished she had warned him that Lady Lawson was a menace.

Lady Lawson gave a little laugh.

"I am sure you are busy," she murmured. "But you cannot be too busy both by day and night for ever. We are determined to give a party so you can meet the charming people who are longing to meet you."

"It's so very kind of you," Alister managed to say, "and I will let you know about Wednesday night when I have looked at my diary. But I am sure that my cousin Georgina and I are booked up for at least a week ahead."

As he spoke her name, Georgina realised that Lady Lawson had not been aware that she was there as she was sitting on the sofa by the door,

"Georgina!" Lady Lawson exclaimed. "Is it really you? I find it hard to recognise you, oh, my dear, what a transformation and all for your dear cousin."

Georgina drew in her breath.

She realised as Lady Lawson spoke that, of course, no one local had ever seen her except dressed as a boy.

For the past few days while she had been showing Alister around, she had almost forgotten herself that she looked different and she was behaving differently too.

Lady Lawson walked towards her.

"It's certainly a change. I suppose we must thank your cousin, who has done what none of us dared to do and tell you to look as God made you and not as you distorted yourself into being."

There was nothing Georgina could think of to say.

Without waiting for an answer Lady Lawson turned back to Alister.

"I don't wish to disturb you," she told him. "I only dropped in to tell you how delighted we are that someone so young and so handsome should be at The Castle. My husband remembers your father and mother and is longing to talk to you about the old days when your mother was undoubtedly the belle of every ball."

She paused for a moment and then carried on,

"If you cannot come on Wednesday, then we must arrange another date."

She glanced at the clock before she added,

"I must not stop now. I only popped in on my way to the Lord Lieutenant, who is giving a party for his eldest son's twenty-first birthday."

She did not wait for Alister to answer, but turned again towards Georgina.

"I don't expect you were asked," she said, "because the Lord Lieutenant said long ago he did not know whether to address his letter as 'Miss' or 'Master' and you cannot blame him for that!"

She laughed at her own joke and then she walked towards the door.

There was nothing Alister could do but open it for her and, because it was polite, he had to walk with her down the passage to the hall where a footman hurried to open the front door.

"I cannot get over Georgina's transformation," she told Alister. "It's certainly an improvement and, of course, it has taken place for your benefit."

She looked round the Great Hall almost as if she was seeing it for the first time.

Then she asked,

"Surely she is not staying here without a chaperone, especially now that she is dressed as she should be."

Alister held out his hand.

"Goodbye, Lady Lawson. It's very kind of you to call on me. But I am sure that you and your husband will understand that following my uncle's death there is a great deal for me to think about here before I can consider my own interests."

"We will be very disappointed if we cannot give a party for you soon," Lady Lawson replied. "Of course I understand you are in mourning. Perhaps if you feel like that we should wait a week or so."

"You are very kind and understanding, ma'am."

She walked down the steps, feeling for his arm as she did so and he felt obliged to give it to her until she reached her carriage.

When she had stepped in, she waved her gloved hand to him as the horses moved off.

Alister walked into the house and, without speaking to anyone in the hall, he went back into the study.

Georgina was still sitting at the tea table and she looked up as he came in.

"Has she gone?" she asked.

"She has left, but I want to know what she meant by saying that your appearance had changed completely. She referred to it again before she left and also pointed out that you should have a chaperone."

"Oh, don't listen to her!" Georgina begged. "Papa hated her and she makes trouble wherever she goes. In fact we managed to avoid her for years. It's only because she wants to show off to the rest of the County that she has persuaded her husband to give a party for you."

"I am not interested in the party," Alister replied, "but in the remarks she made about you. Quite frankly I need an explanation."

Georgina sighed.

"It's all due to that tiresome article in *The Morning Post*. Otherwise I am sure she would not have known that you were here."

"I expect she would have learnt sooner or later," Alister answered, "but I want an explanation as to why she was so astonished at your appearance."

Georgina looked down at the tea table wondering what she should say.

"I want the truth," Alister added unexpectedly.

"Very well. Because Papa did not have a son, he brought me up as a boy. I was dressed as one when I rode with him, shot with him and did everything a boy might have done."

She spoke almost defiantly.

There was then a long silence as if Alister felt it impossible to fully comprehend what had happened.

Then he quizzed,

"Why did you change and become as you are now – a young woman?"

Georgina looked away and did not reply.

Again Alister demanded,

"I want the truth, the real truth!"

"Very well," Georgina whispered in a small voice. "I will tell you the truth. I always behaved, because it made Papa happy, as a boy – which he had longed for."

Her voice faltered a little, but she went on bravely,

"When my aunt, Lady Crawford, discovered where you were and knew that you were returning, she came here to see me."

"What for?" Alister asked.

Georgina realised that he was listening to her every word. His eyes were on her face and she knew that it was impossible to lie to him.

"She wanted to make certain that you understood," she said slowly, "that, as Head of the Family, they were all dependent on you. She thought that I would be the only person you would listen to as soon as you arrived and so she told me to be a woman and behave as a woman."

"It really is the most extraordinary story I have ever heard!" Alister exclaimed. "In fact I can hardly believe it is not some fanciful tale from a novel."

"I have told you the truth," she replied sullenly, "which is what you have asked for."

"Are you really saying that all these years you have been growing up you have been treated as a boy?"

"I had what you would call a boy's education from male Tutors and, as I have already said, I did everything with Papa. I helped him to run the estate and I suppose he managed to forget that, because I was dressed as a boy – and behaved like one, he had no heir – as he longed for."

She stumbled over the words, but they were said.

Alister walked across the room and stood with his back to her.

Because she felt that he was hostile, she pleaded,

"Please, please don't be angry. It's just that the whole family was so afraid, as you have lived abroad for so long, that you would not understand your responsibilities here in England."

There was silence and then Alister turned round.

"One thing is quite clear," he insisted. "You cannot stay here with me without a chaperone."

"So that is the idea Lady Lawson put in your head," Georgina replied. "She always was a dreadful trouble-maker. Only she would think that I needed a chaperone when we are cousins."

"Cousin or no cousin, you are a young woman and you cannot live here alone with me. It's something that I should have realised when I first arrived.

Georgina drew in her breath.

"But where can I go?" she asked.

Alister did not answer and after a moment she said,

"If you turn me out, I did think of asking you if I could go to the Dower House. It's in a bad state of repair, but it would be a roof over my head – even if it leaks."

She added the last words almost desperately.

"You must move into the Dower House at once," he said abruptly, "in case other people call on me, which they undoubtedly will."

"But perhaps, if I could stay here in The Castle, we could find – a suitable chaperone," Georgina suggested in a frightened little voice. "It's my home and I will not know – what to do entirely alone."

She thought as she spoke that, if she once left The Castle, Alister would not want her to be involved in any way with the estate.

She would then have nothing to do and the whole idea was terrifying.

"Now let me make this quite clear," Alister said in a cold hard voice she had not heard before. "I had, as you know, an extremely unhappy marriage. I was pressured into it when I was very young by members of the family who thought that they knew what was good for me better than I knew myself."

"I heard you were unhappy," Georgina murmured.

"As you know I went abroad," Alister went on, where I enjoyed myself enormously. I have returned now because it is my duty to look after the estate and, as you have pointed out to me, also the family."

"You did say that it is all very enjoyable – "

"That is for me to decide," Alister retorted, "but one thing is very obvious – you cannot stay here alone with me without damaging your reputation and setting a trap for me which I have every intention of avoiding."

"I don't understand – what you are saying."

"It is quite obvious, from what Lady Lawson said, that I should be pressured, whether I like it or not, into offering you marriage because we have been alone here in what was for many years your home."

Now he was speaking firmly and his voice seemed almost to ring out in the room.

"I am well aware," Alister went on, "that sooner or later either the family or busybodies like Lady Lawson will demand I marry you to save your reputation. So let me make it very clear I have no intention of marrying anyone."

"Of course not – unless you fall in love," Georgina answered. "Then I would naturally – have to leave The Castle for you and your wife, but I thought, as I was useful to you – I could stay until that happened."

"The answer is '*no*'," Alister replied. "I know the tricks and the way a man can be persuaded into doing what he has no wish to do all too well. You must leave here and I will give you money to go anywhere you want."

"But I have always lived here at The Castle," she repeated. "If I go to London or anywhere else, I will be alone and it will be very very frightening."

"You have plenty of relatives. In fact according to the amount I have to pay, there are plenty of them."

"They don't want me," Georgina replied pitifully. "Papa did not invite them here and I have not met many of them except at funerals when Papa felt obliged to put in an appearance."

"So he gave them the money they were asking for and washed his hands of them," Alister stated.

"That is not true. He was very kind when they came to him with their troubles. He advised them whenever he was asked to do so and, as I said, he attended their funerals even if he did not always go to their weddings."

"Did you accompany him dressed as a boy?"

"Of course not! I stayed here and then Papa made excuses as to why I was not with him."

Alister did not reply and after a moment she said,

"I suppose that only people in the County and on the estate knew I was the son Papa did not have. It made him extremely happy and that was more important than anything else."

"I can understand in a way you doing what he wanted, but now he is no longer here and you have become a woman, which you might have found rather difficult after being a boy for so long, you must go away. Even if you do not trap me personally, the scandal, talk and laughter of the family and of the locals will be difficult for me to combat."

"May I please stay in the Dower House?" Georgina begged. "At least then I will feel at home whereas if I go anywhere else I will be entirely alone."

There was silence.

Then she thought that he was about to say 'no', so she carried on,

"Please, please let me stay here, at least until I can find something to do elsewhere. As you know, you have a house in London and if I go there I might be talked about even more than I will be here."

"You must have some relative who will be prepared to have you," Alister replied. "What about Lady Crawford herself, who persuaded you to dress up on my account?"

"Lady Crawford has a large family of her own and she has always disapproved of the way that Papa brought me up," Georgina explained. "I could not bear to hear her finding fault with him as she undoubtedly would."

She paused for a moment before she added,

"Anyway she would not want me and, even if you paid her extra to have me, she would resent me intruding on her family."

"And who could blame her?"

Alister walked back to the window and stood once again gazing out.

There was a long pause before Georgina said,

"I will go to the Dower House tomorrow and I am afraid it will want a great deal doing to it as it is in a very poor state of repair. But I daresay I can find a couple of women from the village to look after me until the rooms are more or less habitable."

"Very well, if that is where you wish to go, then I must agree," he replied, turning from the window. "At the same time I hope that you will make the effort to find something else which is not on top of The Castle, where it will not raise the attention of our family and neighbours."

As he finished speaking, he walked out of the study shutting the door behind him.

Georgina put her hands up to her face.

She could hardly believe that what she had heard was really true.

That she was to leave her home and everything she loved and go to the Dower House which was, she believed, uninhabitable.

It was so like Lady Lawson to come in and create trouble, so much trouble that now her life was turned topsy-turvy.

'There is nothing I can do but leave, as Alister has told me to do,' she said to herself. 'But it will be very very lonely without anyone to talk to.'

Suddenly she put her hands up to her eyes.

"Oh, Papa, why did you have to die? We were so happy and had planned so many marvellous things to do together."

There was no answer, only the quiet of an empty room.

She felt as if she was utterly and completely alone in a world where there was no longer any love or even a kindly word.

CHAPTER SIX

Georgina packed a few clothes, thinking that once she was settled there would be a place for them to hang.

Then she would send for the rest or perhaps would go herself to The Castle when Alister was not at home.

Because she was frightened that, if she had to speak to him again, she might say a lot of things she would later regret, so she went out through the back door to the stables.

She supposed that she would be able to ride her own horse in the future, but at the moment she was not certain of anything, but felt that her whole world had fallen beneath her feet.

She reached the Dower House and opened the door with a key she had brought from her bedroom.

There was a stale smell where the windows had not been opened for ages and everywhere was thick with dust.

She walked into the drawing room, which at one time had been very beautiful, but now the windows were so dirty that it was difficult to see through them.

She knew that it would take days or perhaps weeks to clean all the rooms.

Now she went to look at the bedroom which would be hers and it seemed to her even worse than the rest of the house.

'How can I stay here?' she asked herself.

She went downstairs again, having put her case that carried her clothes down on the floor.

The kitchen seemed slightly cleaner than the rest of the house, although she might have been imagining it.

Then she suddenly realised that she had nothing to eat for her dinner.

'I cannot bear it,' she thought. 'I will have to go to a Posting inn or perhaps ask the Vicar to have me for the night.'

Then there was a knock on the door and she went to open it. To her surprise it was Dawson holding a tray.

"When I heard you'd left, my Lady," he said, "I knew you'd want somethin' for dinner."

"Oh, Dawson," she cried with a break in her voice, "you are the only person who has thought of me. I cannot bear this dirty empty house."

"Now don't you upset yourself, my Lady," Dawson said. "Things'll be better soon and it's just like that Lady Lawson to stir up trouble."

He walked into the kitchen as he spoke and then he put the tray he was carrying down on the kitchen table.

There were silver covers over the dishes which now might be cold, but at least would be well cooked and tasty.

"I've sent to the village," Dawson told her, "for two women who'll give you a hand tonight. Tomorrow I'll ask for someone to clean up the whole place."

Georgina gave a laugh.

"Oh, Dawson, you are so wonderful. I might have known you would come to my rescue. I was just feeling that I must run away to a Posting inn rather than stay here with all this dirt and dust."

"It won't look so bad for long," Dawson promised. "I'll soon get it clean for you and the Missus'll cook you somethin' nice every day till you have time to find a cook."

Georgina wiped away the tears in her eyes.

"You are very kind, Dawson. I am so miserable leaving my home and everything I love."

"I can understand that, my Lady, but you can make this place as pretty as it was in your grandfather's time. At least his Lordship'll have to pay for that."

"I hope he will, but I need to find out how much money I have myself."

"If you asks me," Dawson went on, "there be a lot of things at The Castle that belong to you. So don't you leave them behind, you move them in here. If you're hardup, there are pictures and your mother's jewellery which'll keep you goin' in the way you've been brought up."

Georgina wiped her eyes.

"I feel better – simply because you are here and I know that you will look after me," she whispered. "I hope I will be allowed to ride the horses."

"Well, two of them at any rate were given to you by your father," Dawson said. "One for your birthday and one for Christmas."

"I had forgotten that," Georgina replied. "I am so used to feeling that everything in the home was part of me, it's difficult to remember that it's now his Lordship's."

"If you asks me his Lordship'll feel ever so lonely when you're not there," Dawson remarked.

"He hates women because he was so unhappy when he was married," Georgina explained. "Therefore you will have to find him a man to talk to, otherwise I think he will be as lonely as I will be in the long dark evenings."

Before Dawson could reply there was a knock on the door and he went to answer it.

"Good evening, Mrs. Kershaw and Mrs. Jones. I were just telling her Ladyship you'd not fail to help her."

"Of course we'll 'elp her," Mrs. Kershaw piped up. "but it'll be easier to do things in the mornin'."

"As her Ladyship has to stay here tonight," Dawson said, "if you just concentrate on makin' up a bed for her in her bedroom, I'll give the dinin' room a dust and then we can leave the rest until tomorrow."

The two women laughed.

"That's just like you, it is, Mr. Dawson, to have everythin' at your fingertips," Mrs. Kershaw smiled. "And of course we'll 'ave to do what you tells us. But with a little 'elp we'll soon 'ave this 'ouse lookin' decent. We can't 'ave 'er Ladyship sittin' in a pigsty!"

Then Mrs. Kershaw and Mrs. Jones took some old brushes out of a cupboard and went towards the door.

"Is the linen cupboard locked?" Mrs. Jones asked Dawson as she passed him.

"It must have been at one time," he replied, "but it's my guess that the locks and bolts have mostly rusted and fallen off."

"If you 'ear a shout you'll 'ave to find the key," Mrs. Jones told him.

Dawson turned to Georgina,

"Now you cheer up, my Lady, we can't have you upset. You'll enjoy makin' this house, with no expense spared, just as it ought to be."

Georgina thought that perhaps Alister would refuse to pay and then she told herself that if he did she would sell some of her own treasures.

Dawson took the tray into the dining room and she heard him dust the table and shake the curtains before she went in to see if it was as bad as the drawing room.

Actually it seemed a little better although the carpets needed beating and everything on the sideboard was dusty.

"I'm sure you'd agree," Dawson suggested, "that this'd look better with a coat of paint, my Lady. I never did like that dull colour and if you takes my advice you'll make the whole place bright and clean for yourself."

"I will certainly try," Georgina replied.

"I'm goin' to lay the table for you," Dawson said. "Then, as you know, I has to go back to his Lordship."

He paused for a moment as if to prevent himself from saying something rather rude and then he went on,

"I thinks after all you've been through you should go to bed early tonight. But tomorrow I'll be round to bring your breakfast and make sure that Mrs. Kershaw and Mrs. Jones have turned up with their friends to help them."

"I cannot begin to thank you, Dawson. I was so unhappy before you came that all I wanted to do was to run away."

"That don't sound at all like you, my Lady. You've faced problems before and I knows you'll face them again. Things might not be as bad as you think at the moment. When the sun's shinin' tomorrow, I think some new ideas will come to you. Your father, as you well knows, would never expect a child of his to run away from the enemy!"

Georgina laughed.

"You are quite right, Dawson. Although I am sure we will get into trouble if we refer to his Lordship as the enemy!"

Dawson did not reply at once and then he said,

"Tomorrow I'll come and have a look to see what there is in the cellar. I've a feelin' there's a bottle or two of champagne which'll cheer you up no end."

"You have cheered me up without the champagne," Georgina assured him. "Thank you! Thank you for your kindness."

"You eat up all the Missus prepared for you, then just go upstairs and close your eyes and it'll be mornin' before you can say 'Jack Robinson'."

"I only hope that's true," Georgina murmured. "As you say I am sure I will feel stronger and better tomorrow."

Dawson looked at his watch.

"I'd better be goin', my Lady. I'll just have a word with them two upstairs and then I'll be off."

"Thank you so much, Dawson," Georgina repeated. "I promise you I will try not to be depressed until you come again."

"That's a promise I'd hope you'll keep," Dawson answered as he always had the last word.

As it was nearly dinnertime, Georgina sat down at the table and looked at the dishes Dawson had brought her.

They were all very edible, but she thought far too much for her to eat tonight and the rest would certainly do for luncheon tomorrow.

Then she heard Dawson come downstairs and go out through the front door and she guessed that he was in a hurry to go back in case his Lordship made trouble for him because he was not in The Castle.

Later, when she had eaten her dinner, she heard the two women leaving and she thought it would be a mistake to talk to them.

She was quite certain that the whole village would know in the next hour or two that she had been turned out of The Castle.

She was sure that several of her father's employees would want to help her, but she must be careful not to start a feud between the Castle and the Dower House.

Now that everyone had gone the house seemed very quiet and she found that Dawson had left her a lighted oil lamp in the hall.

When she went up to the bedroom, she found that it was lit with a number of candles and the bed had been made and the dressing table dusted.

The two women had also unpacked her case and the small amount of clothes she had brought with her were hanging in the wardrobe.

'The sooner I go to sleep,' Georgina told herself, 'the sooner tomorrow will come. I must make plans as to which rooms are to be made habitable and then how many people I will employ to paint the whole house. I must also get the roof repaired and a great number of other things that have broken over the years.'

She undressed and climbed into bed, finding that it was surprisingly comfortable.

At the same time there were so many thoughts in her head that it was impossible to sleep.

Quite suddenly she remembered that nearly every night she had read a prayer from a book her mother had once given her.

It consisted of prayers that were said all over the world and they were many prayers from practically every religion translated into English.

It had been beside her mother's bed ever since she could remember and now she longed for it, but realised in the rush of coming away that she had not taken it out of the drawer by her bed.

There were also several other religious books that her mother had treasured. They were in the writing desk in the boudoir leading off her bedroom.

It had always been her mother's room before she had died and Georgina had moved into it simply because she felt that her mother's influence was still there.

The love she had given her since the day she was born was something precious that she was afraid of losing.

'I must collect my Prayer Book,' she decided.

Then she was suddenly scared in case now she had left that Alister who hates women would destroy some of her treasures especially those in her boudoir.

'I must go and bring them here now,' she thought.

It was an impulse that somehow she felt compelled to obey.

She jumped out of bed and found hanging up in the wardrobe a pair of trousers that she had worn when she was dressed as a boy. She slipped them on and found a jumper that went over them.

Without worrying about anything else, she then ran down the stairs and out through the front door which she had forgotten to lock when she went to bed.

It was not far to The Castle.

A new moon was shining, but it did seem a little darker than it usually was.

But she knew every inch of the ground surrounding The Castle.

She also knew how she could go into the back of the building without anyone being aware of it. There was a window that should have been mended a long time ago, but it had been forgotten.

Only last week she had mentioned to Dawson that the next time the carpenter was free he should attend to it.

"He's very busy repairin' the roof at the moment," Dawson had replied. "The rain came in last week and if we're not careful we'll have the whole place awash."

"Well, don't forget to tell him when he has time to see to the one at the back," Georgina had told him.

As she walked under the stars and The Castle was looming up in front of her, she thought,

'This is my home and nowhere else, not even if it was Heaven would it mean quite so much to me.'

She thought of all the days when she had been so happy with her father and just how much they had enjoyed riding together and it seemed horrible and unfair that The Castle which had been her home since she was born was no longer open to her.

'I must try to arrange to collect everything I own personally,' she determined as she turned towards the back entrance.

She only wished that she could have one tower of The Castle for herself, but she knew that was impossible and she was certain that Alister would resent her coming and going.

'I expect eventually,' she thought, 'he will turn me out of the Dower House as well. Then I will have to leave and go to somewhere where I know no one.'

Because the idea was really depressing, she forced herself to try to think of what she should take away at the moment besides the Book of Prayers.

She found that the shutter was open and so was the window behind it because the catches were broken.

It was not difficult for her to pull them open and crawl in.

Everything was dark and eerily silent.

She knew that, as the footmen's quarters were upstairs and Dawson and his wife slept on the other side of the kitchen, no one would hear her.

Nevertheless she took off her shoes and left them by the window and then she walked slowly up the stairs in her stockinged feet thinking it was so quiet that even the mice must be asleep.

She reached the first floor and this, of course, was dangerous. It was possible, although unlikely, that Alister was moving about.

However, she was sure by this time that he would be in the Master suite and fast asleep. He had said that he liked going to bed early so that it was easier to get up early.

Georgina thought that it must be about two o'clock in the morning by now and he would therefore certainly not be expecting visitors nor would he hear her walking silently down the passage that led to the first floor.

Her room was some distance from the Master suite and, as she opened the door, she saw that the curtains had not been pulled.

Moonlight was streaming into the room from the window and it looked even more beautiful than it had in the daytime.

Because it had been hers and her mother's before her, she felt herself throb with unhappiness because from this moment on she had no right to be in it.

She could remember so clearly her mother looking exceedingly beautiful, even though she was so ill, lying in the large canopied bed.

And she could recall the flowers her mother had loved that scented the room, making it look so enchanting.

As Georgina walked from the bed to the dressing table, she wondered if it would be possible for her to spirit away the mirror with its golden cupids climbing up it.

It was an *objet d'art* she had loved as a child and she remembered when she was small how she would stare at herself in it so she could see her face reflected between the cupids.

She found the book she wanted in the drawer of the table by her bed and the other books that her mother had prized were in the boudoir.

She opened the communicating door and, just as in the bedroom, because there was no one sleeping there, the curtains were not drawn.

Actually she had no need for light to take her to the writing table standing between the windows that looked out over the garden.

She opened the drawer and found the two books she particularly wanted.

Then she was aware that lying beside them was the small revolver that her father had given her as a present the Christmas before he died.

It was an improvement on the duelling pistol she had used when she was practising with him on a target in the garden and he had made her use it on several crows that she had brought down easily.

"A woman should be able to defend herself," he had told her. "I want you, when you travel, to take this with you. It's light and takes up very little room and will protect you against highwaymen or anyone else who tries to take advantage of you."

"It's a lovely present, Papa, and I am absolutely thrilled with it," Georgina had enthused.

She thought as the revolver was so light and yet so easy to use that she would certainly take it with her the next time they went on a long journey to the North or even, although her father might disapprove, to London.

As she took it out, she realised that it was loaded and there was also a box full of bullets, which she would need if she used it.

'I am certainly not going to leave this for Alister,' she said to herself. 'I wonder what else there is which is very precious and I could not bear to part with.'

She opened one or two drawers and found several photographs and a miniature of her mother that she thought she would take with her rather than wait for the servants to pack them in case they felt they were of no significance.

As she picked up the revolver, she was thinking how carefully her father had taught her to handle it.

And how pleased she had been when he said – and it was the biggest compliment he could ever pay her – that she shot as well as any man.

She felt that her father would be hurt and upset at the idea of her having to leave The Castle, but there was no point in arguing with Alister, who had obviously made up his mind about her.

Even if she had suggested having a chaperone, he was not going to agree.

'I am just an exile from everything I love,' she told herself miserably.

Then suddenly to her surprise she heard a man's voice shouting,

"What the hell do you think you are doing?"

As Georgina jumped to her feet realising that it was Alister speaking, she heard a shot.

It seemed to echo and re-echo round the walls.

Then she heard a second shot and, running to the door that led into the passage, she opened it.

She saw as she did so that Alister was hanging over the stairs halfway down them.

As she stared at him, he fell backwards and crashed onto the stairs themselves.

She ran over to the balustrade on the landing and, looking down, she saw three men.

One of the men was carrying a gun and he had obviously shot her cousin with it.

The other two were carrying a huge picture which came from the drawing room. And it was one of the finest works Fragonard had ever painted and it was too large to go through the diamond-paned windows.

The men who were stealing it were now carrying it towards the front door which Georgina could see was ajar.

Then, as the man with the gun pointed it through the banisters and it was obvious that he was going shoot Alister again, Georgina pointed her revolver at him.

She pulled the trigger as her father had taught her.

She hit the man in the shoulder.

He gave a scream of pain and fell to the ground, his gun falling from his hand.

Then the two men carrying the picture looked up at him, dropped it and ran to the front door.

Georgina fired at them, hitting one man in the leg and the other in the back.

As they fell screaming onto the steps, she ran down the stairs to where Alister was lying.

She could see, as she reached him, that his face was covered with blood and it must have been from the second shot the man had fired.

He was unconscious.

It was then, as she looked through the open door, she could see in the bright moonlight a covered cart outside drawn by two horses.

A man who had obviously been in charge of them was running towards the man who had collapsed on top of the marble steps.

The intruder she had shot in the leg was gasping,

"Get me away. Get me away before they find me!"

Georgina looked down and saw Dawson, who had obviously heard the shots, coming from the kitchen and he was wearing a black dressing gown.

"They have shot his Lordship, Dawson! And he is unconscious!"

"The devils were stealing one of our best pictures," Dawson cried angrily, pushing the Fragonard to one side.

"They are all wounded," Georgina told him, "but it would be wiser to let them get away."

Dawson, who had reached the front door, saw that the second man Georgina had shot was crawling down on his hands and knees. Another man was being half-carried and half-dragged towards the cart.

"If they've killed his Lordship," Dawson cried, "they'll hang for it!"

"He is still unconscious and losing a lot of blood," Georgina cried, "but he is not dead. If it is known that people can break into the house and steal pictures so easily, it might happen again."

"I see what you mean," Dawson replied. "I'll just go and get Lever and he'll help me carry his Lordship up to his bed."

Georgina looked down at Alister.

She wished that she had a handkerchief to wipe his face.

Then she saw that there was one in the pocket of the long black robe he was wearing.

She wiped the side of his head and face.

She could see that the bullet had cut a line from the side of his cheek up to his forehead.

But she was certain that the bullet had not entered his head.

Blood was also coming from his arm, but there was no point in her trying to prevent it from doing so.

She merely crouched down on the stairs beside him and thanked God that he had not been killed by the thieves.

Dawson had left the door open and she could see the last wounded man being helped by the driver into the back of the cart with the other men lying on the floor.

As the cart drove away, she thought that she had been wise in letting the thieves go.

They must have seen the lengthy description of the treasures of The Castle in the newspaper just as Lady Lawson had done and then they had doubtless learnt in the village that there were only a few servants in The Castle.

Alister was still lying with his eyes closed when Dawson came back with Lever.

He was a sturdy man who brought in the coal and wood when it was wanted and he was capable of doing any job requiring strength and perseverance.

He and Dawson picked up Alister without too much difficulty and carried him to his bedroom.

There was only one candle by the bed and Alister had obviously lit it when something had alerted him to the fact that there were people moving about downstairs.

While Dawson and Lever put Alister down on the bed and pulled off his dressing gown to look at his arm, Georgina lit the other candles in the room.

It was then easier to see the wound the thief had made.

It was halfway up his arm and Georgina knew that he had actually been aiming at Alister's heart.

If he had hit it, it would have killed him.

As it was the blood was pouring from his wound and the gash on his head was also bleeding.

She ran to the kitchen to fetch hot water to bathe his wounds and then she woke Mrs. Dawson and told her that they wanted bandages urgently.

When she got back, Alister was comfortably in bed.

But his arm was still bleeding as was the wound on his head, which was deeper than she had at first thought.

"He might have been killed by either of the shots!" Dawson exclaimed.

"I know," Georgina replied. "He must have heard them and gone to see what was happening without realising they were thieves."

She looked down at Alister and said,

"We must send for a doctor."

"Yes, of course, my Lady. Lever will fetch the one in the village and the sooner he comes here the better."

Lever, who was bending over Alister, rose to his feet.

"I'll be as quick as I can," he said, "but I makes no promises as to 'ow long I'll be."

"You can run when it suits you," Dawson retorted, "so just hurry. The Master's lost too much blood for it to be healthy."

They tried to bandage his arm, but it was difficult and, despite all the layers they put on it, the blood seeped through.

Georgina wiped Alister's other wound very gently, but that too continued to bleed.

His eyes did not open and several times she stopped and listened to be quite certain he was actually breathing.

*

It was nearly two hours later that the doctor arrived. He lived in the village, but he had been attending a birth to one of the farmers' wives.

He was horrified, as Georgina knew he would be, to learn that the thieves had broken into The Castle so easily and that they almost got away with a valuable Fragonard and perhaps a number of other pictures.

She was to learn later that one of the men had taken two of the best miniatures away with him, but they had fallen from his pocket when he was crawling down the steps outside and they had therefore got away with nothing.

The doctor was appalled to find that Alister was in such a poor condition.

"If this shot had gone two inches to the left," he exclaimed, "it would undoubtedly have hit his heart and he would be dead."

"What can we do about it?" Georgina asked.

The doctor smiled at her.

"It is what *you* can do," he emphasised. "You know as well as I do that there is no nurse in this village and it's impossible for me to find one."

"You want me to nurse him?" Georgina asked.

"You nursed your father better than anyone else could have done," he replied, "and I know how good you are. So it is up to you to save him."

"You mean the wound is dangerous?"

"Yes. It is very deep and he has lost an enormous amount of blood," the doctor replied. "The wound on his face which has rendered him unconscious may keep him in such a condition for some time."

"Of course I will do anything you tell me."

"Well, it's going to be very hard work," the doctor replied, "but you are used to that. You will have to sleep as near as possible to him in case he wakes in the night. The one thing he must not do is to start his wound bleeding again."

"I understand," Georgina answered.

"Tell them to make up a bed for you in his sitting room. If you keep the communicating door open, you will hear him murmur, just as you listened for your father you will have to listen for him."

"I will do exactly as you say, but please come back early tomorrow morning and if you can find a nurse – "

The doctor threw up his hands.

"Where am I going to find one who is as good as you are? In fact as far as we are concerned in this village there is only you and you!"

Georgina smiled.

"I will do my best. You know I will, but I am very worried about him,"

"So am I, as it happens," the doctor admitted. "But we will win through as we always do."

He smiled at her and patted her on the shoulder before he left.

"You are a good girl and, as it happens, a very good nurse. I thought when you were nursing first your mother and then your father that I could do with you. I could give you a thousand patients if you had time to attend to them!"

Georgina laughed.

"I seem to manage to find them myself and I only hope that my cousin will not be ill for very long."

The doctor shrugged his shoulders.

"He is going to be most uncomfortable for quite some time and it's bad luck after he has just arrived at The Castle. It's a good thing you are here and then everything will run smoothly, but you still need to look out for more thieves."

"That is just what I was thinking," she replied.

She waited until the doctor had gone, then realised that Dawson was waiting for her.

He came from under the stairs to say,

"So you'll not be moving to the Dower House now, my Lady."

"I suppose not. You heard the doctor say I have to sleep in his Lordship's sitting room and I expect the bed I used when Papa was so ill is not far away."

Dawson smiled.

"It seems Fate that you shouldn't leave us," he said, "and I'll bring your cases back from the Dower House early tomorrow."

Georgina thought for a moment and then said,

"All the same I think that the women who you were kind enough to find for me should go on with their work. I am sure that the moment his Lordship is better he will want me to go back to the Dower House."

"Well, it certainly gives us more time to breathe and make it a place you'll be proud of, my Lady."

"I will leave it to you, Dawson, but now for tonight at any rate I will sit in the armchair in his Lordship's room just in case he wakes up and wonders what has happened."

"I'll bring you some blankets and an eiderdown, my Lady. If you puts your feet up on one of them stools you'll be comfortable enough until we bring in a bed tomorrow."

"Thank you, Dawson," Georgina answered.

She went back into the bedroom to look at Alister and thought that he had gone very pale.

Dawson brought in all she needed to make her more comfortable and because she could not see or hear him she moved the armchair quite close to Alister's bed so that she would be aware of any movement he made.

Then Dawson brought her a cup of tea and she thanked him for it.

"Now don't you worry," he assured her. "If he gets any worse or you wants any help, then you ring the bell. I don't sleep heavy and I'll come if you wants me."

"I know you will and thank you very much."

She asked him to blow out all the candles except for the one by the bed. It gave enough light for her to see how Alister was looking or if he had moved in any way.

As the door shut behind Dawson, she thought how strange it was that she had come back to fetch her mother's Book of Prayers the very moment she was needed.

It was almost as if God and the angels were looking after Alister to make sure that he was not deprived of the treasures of The Castle accumulated over the centuries.

'They might easily have killed him,' she mused, 'if I had not intervened.'

It seemed almost like a miracle that she had just found her revolver and been able to save his life.

If his orders had been obeyed, she would have been in the Dower House and not aware of anything that was happening until the morning, in which case it would have been far too late.

As she settled herself down and closed her eyes, she told herself that this could easily happen again.

After all that had been written in the newspapers, there must be thieves all over the country who would read it and they would realise that here were pictures, china and silver all waiting for the taking.

'We really must be properly protected,' Georgina told herself before she fell into an exhausted sleep.

CHAPTER SEVEN

Georgina took charge as if she had been her father.

Dawson was told to find five footmen all who had been in the Army and were used to handling a gun.

The two scullions employed in the kitchen and who brought in the coal were ex-Army men.

She increased the number of housemaids until there were enough to open all the rooms that had been closed and clean them thoroughly for the first time in years.

She herself nursed Alister and, as the doctor had ordered, she slept in the sitting room with the door open so that she could hear if he woke in the night.

He was, however, suffering from loss of blood and the wound in his head made him oblivious of everything.

Looking at him lying in bed so handsome and so strong in himself, it seemed to Georgina horrifying that he should suffer like this from those three dastardly thieves and there was no chance, the doctor told her, of having any help in nursing him.

"There is no one in the village I would trust with an ill cat, let alone a human being," he had said. "It would be a mistake to bring someone down from London who was not used to the country."

"Of course it would be and would upset the whole staff," Georgina replied. "I promise I can manage very well just as I did with Papa."

"And your mother," he pointed out. "You are born to be a perfect nurse even if you are not aware of it."

Georgina smiled at him.

"You have been a marvellous doctor ever since I can remember and you must now save my cousin Alister."

"Of course I will save him or rather *you* will," the doctor replied almost crossly. "I have never had such a fit or strong-boned patient before and I have no intention of him going to Heaven earlier than expected."

"I think that is a compliment and, of course, I am sure you will save him," Georgina laughed.

"We *will* save him," he said, accentuating the word.

She knew that meant she was on duty for twenty-four hours a day, but she did not mind.

She was really determined that Alister should not be permanently injured by the thieves.

She blamed her father and herself for not thinking before that this might happen. But how could they know that someone in London would write in the newspapers about the treasures that would draw the attention of every thief in England?

Because she was so desperately worried she added two nightwatchmen to the steadily increasing staff and they too promised that they were exceedingly handy with a gun.

"You must always take one with you," Georgina told them, "if you have to sleep, then sleep in the daytime."

They laughed at this and said they would be awake at night and that she was not to worry.

But of course she worried and she worried too over Alister.

The doctor said that it was natural for someone who had lost a great deal of blood and was badly wounded to be unconscious.

"It's the same as having a stroke," he advised, "and he will wake up when you least expect it."

It was on the first night after the burglary that she recalled something that had been at the back of her mind all the time the doctor was talking.

It was her father who had once said that, when a person suffered a stroke, if they were talked to, it helped their recovery. Also, although it seemed strange, they were aware of it despite being deeply unconscious.

It was a piece of information that had remained at the back of her mind.

Now she was certain that she should talk to Alister and bring him back to consciousness.

She could not help thinking that when he did so he might be furious with her for employing so many people, but at the same time she was certain that they were needed and that he could afford it.

In fact the day after the burglary she asked Mr. Milton who did the accounts for the whole estate to tell her exactly how much money her cousin had inherited.

"I don't think I ought to tell you that, my Lady," Mr. Milton said with embarrassment.

"As a lot of it is my money and it was Papa's when he was alive, I think I am entitled to know how much I can spend, also if I am spending too much."

It was an argument Mr. Milton had no answer to.

He therefore told her exactly what money her father had handled and which had been passed on to Alister.

She was astounded that there was so much, yet they had lived so simply, but then she realised that her father had never had expensive tastes.

As long as he could afford the best horses and had gamekeepers who were certain to provide him with good sport in the winter, he had not wanted to spend money unnecessarily.

Therefore what he had not spent had accumulated as Mr. Milton had pointed out.

There was no doubt at all that Alister could afford not just the staff she had engaged but also to pay for all the repairs required at the Dower House.

She thought that, if they were completed, however much Alister might reproach her for being extravagant, he would not be able to put the house back into the terrible condition it was at the moment.

Mrs. Dawson was delighted to have new help in the kitchen as, in addition to the two scullions, who were badly needed, Georgina supplied her with two other excellent women. They obeyed her every word and admired and praised everything she cooked.

Every morning she ordered food for Alister, but he was still unconscious and unable to eat it.

It therefore went to the dining room and, rather than waste the dishes, she ate them herself. And now that Mrs. Dawson had help, the food at The Castle was undoubtedly superlative.

*

It was in the quiet of the afternoon, when everyone else was resting after a strenuous morning, that she talked to Alister.

She told him exactly what she was doing and why she was doing it and she told him what was happening on the estate and the news from the farmers.

Because they were aware of what was happening at The Castle, they had all come to ask for new equipment, more livestock and for urgent repairs to be carried out to their buildings and Georgina agreed to all they suggested.

Knowing that Alister could not only afford it but it was done before he could interfere.

'Even if he is angry with me,' she thought, 'it will still have benefitted those who have suffered so much during the war.'

They were the people her father had always wanted to help, but thought he must not be extravagant. She could understand it was not because he was mean but that he had been careful over money.

During the war every penny had counted and there were not the men to spend it as they had all been swept away to fight.

Yet now, she told herself, in peace it was different. Prices, which had dropped dismally at the end of the war, were not increasing, but farmers were finding it worthwhile to grow better yielding crops.

She told all this to Alister hoping that he could hear her and she felt that it helped her to work out on her own what she should do for the best.

And her talks with him gave her the feeling that she was not in any way defrauding him.

If he could not hear what she said, it was not her fault, but she fervently believed that he could understand everything he was saying.

She spoke to him in a soft, sweet and gentle voice that he had appreciated so much from his women in the East.

She was honest with him down to the money she had expended on new thatch for the cottages in the village and repairs to the windows in the Church.

She hid nothing from him.

Although, as he did not move or open his eyes, she was sometimes afraid he would die whilst she was talking.

But, when she felt his pulse, it had slowed down as was almost normal and, when she wiped his brow, it was no longer wet with perspiration.

Dawson shaved him every day and perhaps to cheer Georgina up, he invariably said,

"His Lordship's lookin' a lot better and I thinks his breathing's more steady than it were yesterday."

"I am sure you are right, Dawson," she agreed.

However, she knew he was just encouraging her.

Because she thought that perhaps music might help him back to consciousness, she arranged for the piano from the music room to be carried upstairs to his room.

She had learnt to play when she was quite small to please her mother and she had played to her when she was ill until the day she died.

Now she played to Alister the tunes she loved that to her were dreamy and uplifting.

'Surely,' she thought, 'if he can hear nothing else he will hear the lovely tunes that seem to fill the room with light and joy,' and, because some of them were so moving, they brought tears to her eyes.

The doctor came every morning and encouraged her by saying,

"I know you find it hard to understand because he does not move or speak, but his Lordship is much better than he was when I first saw him. I promise you he is on the road to recovery."

"I do hope you are right," Georgina sighed.

"You have been wonderful," the doctor continued. "If you had not been here, I cannot imagine how I would have been able to cope with him."

"But I am still here and he is still in a coma," she said in a worried voice.

"I promise you it's only a question of time," the doctor answered, "then he will be on his feet again and doubtless finding fault with everything you have done!"

There was a twinkle in the doctor's eyes and she realised that he was teasing her.

Equally he was uncomfortably near the truth.

As Alister hated women, he would obviously hate everything she had ordered to be done and in which case everything might go back to how it had been before the burglary.

When she did escape from Alister's room either for her meals or because she felt she must have some fresh air, she was really astonished at what had been achieved in The Castle itself as well as at the Dower House.

The new maids with the help of the footmen had cleaned every room and they looked, Georgina thought, exactly as they had when her mother had been alive.

There were flowers in the drawing room, in fact in all the rooms, even in the passages.

There had been a rather bare boudoir attached to the Master suite which was now a blaze of flowers and they extended into the patient's bedroom as well.

'Perhaps he hates flowers,' Georgina thought as she played the piano to him.

But she knew that they inspired her to play better than she had ever played before.

She thought that such melodies must awaken him to reality, even though she thought at times that he had left this world for good.

That evening, when talking to him, she said softly,

"You must wake up now and see what's happening. You will be surprised, perhaps angry, but The Castle has never looked so beautiful nor has the garden. There were two foals born today and both of them will, I think, be magnificent jumpers as their mother has been."

She paused for a moment before she went on,

"I could not resist a gallop early this morning on one of your faster horses. But he is waiting for you and feeling a bit despised with only a woman on his back. But I am quite certain that he will win every race you enter him for and he needs you as does everyone else on the estate."

She bent forward and touched his cheek gently.

"Wake up, Alister," she whispered. "Do wake up. Your world is very exciting and I pray you will be pleased when you see it and not be angry."

The next day the doctor came again and, having examined his patient, he was even more encouraging than he had been previously.

"His pulse is steady and you will see that he will soon be back in this world again, however much he may be enjoying slipping away from us."

"I hope you are right," Georgina sighed.

That night before she retired to bed she went in as she always did to look at Alister.

The candles burning by his bed and the scent of the flowers seemed almost overwhelming.

She knelt down beside him and murmured,

"Oh, Alister, hurry and wake up. There are such exciting things going on. I have so much to show you."

As she spoke, she wondered if he would disapprove of it and tell her, as he had told her before, that he would not have her in his house.

'Why should he change,' she asked herself, 'just because he has been ill?'

Then, on an impulse, she bent forward and said,

"Get well, even if you are angry with me. It will be better than you lying here looking so handsome, so young and yet you have gone away to some other world where we cannot reach you."

She felt as she spoke that he was like a child who had to be loved to be reassured.

She had talked to him so often and in a way he had become part of her and she now felt entirely responsible for him.

"Get well and come back to us," she whispered.

It was a call that came from the very depths of her heart.

Then, as she rose to go to her room, Alister opened his eyes and she gave a little cry of astonishment.

"Where am – I?" he said in a voice she could hardly hear. "What has – happened?"

"You can speak!" Georgina cried. "Oh, Alister, I thought you would never come back to us."

Her voice broke and there were tears in her eyes as she bent over him.

She felt that he was a child who depended on her and by some miracle she had saved him.

He now looked up at her as if he was seeing her for the first time.

Then he muttered,

"I am – tired. I must go to – sleep."

Georgina drew in her breath and, as she realised that Alister had gone to sleep, she bent forward and very lightly kissed his cheek.

The next morning when the doctor came, she met him on the doorstep to tell him exactly what had happened.

"He spoke and asked where he was," she told him excitedly.

"I came as soon as you sent for me. As I have come without my breakfast, I would be very grateful if I could have something to eat when I have seen our patient."

"But of course," Georgina replied. "I would expect Dawson has thought of that already."

They went upstairs together.

As she now drew back the curtains, Georgina heard Alister replying to the doctor's questions as if he had not been unconscious for so long.

"What – happened – to me?" he asked jerkily.

The doctor smiled.

"You will hear it from your wonderful nurse who has looked after you all the time you have been lying here ignoring our efforts to get you back on your feet."

"I remember some men stealing a picture – "

"That is right," the doctor agreed. "And when you tried to stop them, they shot you. They would have killed you if it had not been for Lady Georgina. She not only saved your life but she kept talking to you every day. No other nurse in the world could have done better."

"I heard her and I heard her music," he answered.

"You will hear a great deal more now that you are fully conscious," the doctor said.

He then gave Georgina and Dawson a number of instructions before he left and said that he would be back early in the afternoon.

"Give him anything he wants," he told them. "He is now on the mend and will soon be his old self again."

He drove away without saying any more.

Georgina thought it meant that she would soon be out of The Castle and back to the Dower House.

Yet somehow she could not believe after she had been so close to him and he meant so much to her that he would do so.

When he then fell asleep, she realised that it was because he was tired and not because he was unconscious as he was breathing quite normally.

When finally she went to bed, she felt that they had passed the crossroads and now he would really improve.

*

Georgina woke early and crept into Alister's room to find that he was still asleep and she thought that it was a normal sleep as it had been last night.

She realised it was not yet six o'clock and the sun was just coming up over the trees.

She had a sudden yearning to be riding.

After yet another look at her patient, she put on her riding clothes and slipped out through the back door of The Castle that led to the stables.

Then ten minutes later she was riding Sunlight over the paddock and into the fields that led to the wood.

Now the sun was in her eyes and the clear fresh air touched her cheeks.

She was thinking that now Alister had come back to normality everything was very wonderful.

At the same time deep in her heart she was afraid, desperately afraid, that once again he would send her away.

She wanted to stay. She wanted to be with him.

She wanted to look after him as she had been doing as if he was a child and not a man who could hurt her and make her desperately unhappy.

She had actually not been to the Dower House for two days and, because Alister was getting better, there was so much to see to in The Castle.

Also she had loved playing to him, telling him with music that he must get well and that the world outside was waiting for him.

'Now I can say it in words,' she reflected.

But she was afraid that he would not want to hear them and that, as soon as he was well enough, he would send her away.

It was then, as she was riding back to The Castle, she admitted to herself that he meant more to her than just a patient the doctor had given her.

She had talked to him not only about the estate but about herself and she had told him secrets that she could not have told anyone else.

Because he had been unconscious she felt he would never remember them and they were safe in his keeping.

As she turned for home, she had a full view of The Castle with the sun glinting on the mullioned windows.

There was just enough breeze to raise the Standard, which was flying from the highest tower, to show that the Earl was in residence.

'My home! The place I love best in all the world,' Georgina sighed to herself.

It was then that she knew, although she hardly dare admit it to herself, she not only loved The Castle but the man who now owned it.

She thought of him as a child who had been injured who wanted her compassion and she had given him not just that but tried with her brain, her heart and her soul to make him well.

She did not know why, but somehow he had drawn from her the very depths of her being.

In giving him her heart, she had lost it.

'How could I be so crazy and so stupid as to love a man who hates me because I am a woman?' she asked herself. 'He turned me away before he was wounded and will turn me away once he is himself again.'

It was something that she had never thought would happen to her but it had.

She had loved him because he was so helpless and she had thought that he might die.

She had loved him because he had been like a child who depended on her.

And in giving back his brain she had also given him everything she owned, in fact herself.

When she reached the steps, she gave her horse to one of the grooms.

"Had a nice ride, my Lady?" he asked.

"Yes, lovely," Georgina replied.

She patted Sunlight and wondered, because it did not belong to her but to Alister, if in the future she would be able to ride him again.

As she walked slowly to the front of The Castle, she recognised that it was part of her heart.

Not only because she had been born there and lived there, but because everything about her was somehow part of The Castle too, not just her body but her brain, her heart, her prayers and in fact all of herself.

She realised now that this was how it had always been, but she had not been able to put it into words, not even to herself, until now.

But she knew that now Alister was better he might send her away again.

She thought that if he did so she would perhaps be able to disobey him.

She could hide in the cellars or in the towers and The Castle was big enough for him never to know that she was there.

But because it was her home and because it was everything she had always loved, now that her father and mother were dead, she felt that she must cling to it.

Otherwise she might as well die.

'If they had shot me instead of Alister,' she mused, 'it would not have mattered particularly.'

Then she knew that was in a way blasphemous.

She had done so much for The Castle just as The Castle had done so much for her.

It could not be dismissed by a bullet from a burglar and nor could she throw it away by saying that she would live elsewhere.

'I love it,' she pondered, looking up at the towers silhouetted against the sky, 'just as I love the man who now owns it although he is not interested in me.'

It was with a tremendous effort that she managed to walk into the hall and smile at the footman who wished her 'good morning'.

Then she went up the stairs and along the corridor that led to the Master suite.

By this time Dawson would have woken Alister, shaved him and brought him his breakfast.

She went first to her own room and changed from her riding habit into one of the pretty dresses that had belonged to one of her cousins.

She tidied her hair and then she went through the communicating door into the Master suite.

She walked towards the bed as she had done every morning.

She gave a little gasp as she realised that the bed was empty and for a moment it went through her mind that something disastrous had happened.

Then, as she turned towards the window, she saw Alister sitting at a table wearing his dressing gown and reading a newspaper.

"You are up!" she managed to cry.

He smiled at her.

"Come and sit down," he said. "I have ordered breakfast for us in the sunshine. Dawson has promised me that I will be able to go downstairs tomorrow as long as I am a good boy and don't do too much today."

"You can really move!" Georgina exclaimed.

"As you can see I have managed to walk here," he replied. "I suggest you eat your breakfast before it gets cold."

Feeling as if she was in a dream, Georgina sat down beside him.

Now the colour was back in his face.

Although he was thinner than he had been before, he was still exceedingly good-looking.

Despite her resolution to be as quiet as possible, she could not help herself from saying,

"I hope you are not doing too much. You must be careful of yourself, Alister."

"I thought that you were begging me to get better quickly as you had so much to show me," Alister replied.

"Did you hear me – say that?" she stammered.

"I knew you were talking to me," he answered. "I did not know at first who it was, but someone was talking to me, pulling me back from somewhere I wanted to go but was unable to do so."

"Did you really feel that?" Georgina asked.

"At first I did not understand what you said when you talked to me," he replied. "But afterwards I had an idea of what it was and I waited for it and, believe it or not, I could hear your every word."

"So you really knew that I was talking to you?"

"Yes, I knew it was you, Georgina."

She remembered the secrets she had told him about herself and the passionate way she had begged him to get well quickly.

Now she felt embarrassed and the colour rose in her cheeks.

As she looked away from him, she had no idea how lovely she looked in the sunshine streaming in through the window.

"You actually told me a great deal while I was unconscious," Alister admitted. "But now I want you to tell me all over again so that I don't miss anything."

"I cannot believe that you really heard me talking to you," Georgina murmured.

"Of course I heard you. I knew that you wanted me and would not let me go to where I wanted to go."

"You really wanted to leave us?"

"I don't know whether it was just something that happened to me," he replied, "or whether my mind told me that I was facing a choice between Heaven and earth."

Then he smiled.

"As you can see, I have chosen earth and now I am asking you to tell me what has happened. I gather both from you and Dawson that much has changed."

"I am not going to tell you now because I think it may be too much for you. As it was impossible to engage a nurse locally, I was the only one to do it so I don't want you to have a relapse."

Alister laughed.

"Now you are eluding me. I am feeling like my old self, except that I am little tired. I know that the doctor told me that I must spend the day in bed, but tomorrow I will be different."

"If you have finished breakfast," she suggested, "I think you should go back to bed now."

"I will do so on one condition."

"What is that?" Georgina asked.

"That you come and talk to me and tell me all the things I could not quite understand when you were saying them before."

"Of course I will do that," she promised, "but let me call Dawson to take you to bed."

"If you help me, we can manage without Dawson," he replied.

He started to rise as he spoke.

Instinctively Georgina rose to her feet and put her arm round his back so that he could rest on her shoulder.

Slowly, very slowly, they walked towards the bed.

As they reached it, she then helped him out of his dressing gown.

As he lay back against the pillows, she pulled the bedclothes over him.

"Now rest," she told him, "and don't worry about anything. Everything is perfect."

"Of course it is," Alister replied, "because you have arranged it. Now I suggest you play to me as you played when I was unconscious."

"You heard the music?" she asked excitedly.

"Of course I heard it and it told me everything I wanted to know even more implicitly than you told me in words."

Georgina gave a little laugh.

"I don't believe this is happening. I prayed and prayed that you would get well, but I did not imagine it would be so quickly."

"And I have a feeling that your prayers are always answered."

"I wish that was true," Georgina murmured.

She walked to the piano and sat down and, without thinking, she played the tunes she had played when he was unconscious.

It must have been a quarter of an hour later that she realised he was fast asleep.

As Dawson came into the room, she put her finger to her lips so that he did not speak.

He picked up the breakfast plates and put them on a tray and took it away.

When he was outside the room, she followed him.

"I think you should send for the doctor," she said.

"He be coming at midday," Dawson replied. "His Lordship's recovered exactly as I knew he would."

"Yes, and so quickly," Georgina agreed.

"That's how it happens, my Lady, and now he'll be up in a few days. If you asks me, he'll be ridin' before the end of the week."

"I don't believe it," Georgina retorted.

"I'm not askin' for a bet on it, as your Ladyship'll lose your money. But it's good news and that's what the doctor'll say when he arrives."

Alister was still asleep when the doctor came and, when Georgina told him all that had happened, he was delighted.

"Now that he is well on the way to recovery," he said, "I can see that my services are no longer needed."

"You saved him!" Georgina exclaimed.

"It is you who have done that, Lady Georgina. And if ever anyone was born to be a nurse by nature that is exactly what you are."

"I suppose it's a compliment," Georgina answered, "but if you are thinking of giving me a new career, I would point out that people like him are the people I have loved."

As she said the last word she drew in her breath and felt herself blush because it came out of her lips without thinking.

But fortunately the doctor was too busy picking up his hat and bag that he had left in the hall to notice.

"I will see you tomorrow morning," he called out, "and don't let our patient do too much too quickly. It's always the same with these men, once they are on their feet they want to be on a horse and it's far too soon for that."

He had gone out to his carriage before she could think of an answer.

Then she ran back upstairs simply because she was so excited and pleased that Alister was really better.

She played the piano to him again and they talked when he was not sleeping.

*

It was the third day after he had recovered before the doctor said that he could go downstairs.

This was what Georgina was frightened of, not only because it might hurt him to do too much too quickly but because she was afraid of what he would say when he saw how many new servants had been engaged.

Also how different the rooms looked since they had been cleaned, polished and decked with flowers.

"Perhaps you had better wait until another day," she suggested when they had breakfasted together.

"What for?" Alister asked. "I am feeling exactly like my old self and I am tired of being an invalid. I want to be downstairs and I want to see the garden. I want to see the new arrivals in the stables."

"How do you know there are new arrivals?" she asked.

"You told me there had been new foals born," he replied, "and also one of the racehorses had twins."

"You really heard me tell you that?"

Alister smiled.

"I admit that Dawson has confirmed it to me."

"Well, if you come downstairs, I will get the horses paraded in front of you, but I am sure that it is too soon for you to go to the stables."

"I might have guessed that you *would* bully me," he laughed.

She could not help thinking that if he had been honest he would have said,

'I might have guessed, as you are a woman, that you *would* bully me.'

But she merely replied meekly,

"I am only saying what is best for you and after all I don't want to nurse you again. I was so afraid I might fail and lose you."

She spoke lightly and Alister asked,

"Would that really have mattered to you?"

Despite an effort not to feel shy, she felt the colour rise in her cheeks.

She was relieved when he did not say anymore.

Both she and Dawson helped him down the stairs and, when he reached the drawing room, he sank down in a comfortable chair saying as he did so,

"Now this room looks as I always thought it ought to look," he remarked.

Georgina looked at him in surprise.

"I was half afraid," she admitted, "that you would be angry that we had opened all the rooms."

"And that you have an Army to protect them?"

"I suppose Dawson told you that."

"He told me that you did the sensible thing and it's something I should have thought of myself. But, of course, that article in the newspaper would attract thieves and I am thankful that we can now meet them on equal terms if nothing else."

"You mean they had the guns when they came to take away the Fragonard?" Georgina questioned.

"Apparently you had one that saved my life," he replied.

Georgina looked away from him, thinking perhaps he would be shocked at a woman using a man's weapon.

He rose to his feet and walked slowly towards the garden and, because she was worried that he might fall, she joined him.

They stood together at the open window looking out at the flowers which gave a riot of colour on either side of the lawn.

In the centre of it the fountain was playing and the water rising towards the sky was the colour of rainbows in the sunshine.

Georgina felt a little throb go through her in case this was a scene that she would have to leave.

As if he knew what she was thinking, Alister said,

"I am Monarch of all I survey, but I am wondering if in the future I will find my Kingdom rather lonely."

"A thousand people are only too willing to share it with you," Georgina replied. "You have only to send them an invitation and your relatives, and I expect your friends, will come any distance to see anything so beautiful and so precious."

"I will still have no one to talk to at night, as you have done and to speak to me with music."

Because she did not understand, Georgina looked at him in a puzzled way.

Then he said very quietly,

"Why did you kiss me when you knew that I could not respond?"

It was a question she had not expected.

Although she wanted to turn away so that he could not make her answer it, he put his hand on her shoulder.

"You kissed me," he said, "and I knew that you had done so, even though at that moment I could not move. Why did you kiss me?"

She wanted to hide her face, but his arm held her firmly.

She could only look down and stammer,

"I did not know – you were aware of it."

"But I *was* fully aware of it. I think it was that kiss which brought me back to life and, of course, to you."

She looked up at him in surprise and there was an expression in his eyes she had not seen before.

"I suppose you know what you have done to me," he said very quietly.

"What have I done?"

"You have made me fall in love," he replied. "It was something I had vowed never to do."

Georgina drew in her breath.

149

"I don't know what you are saying."

"I think you do," he insisted, "because you kissed me, it is now my turn to kiss you."

He pulled her close to him.

As his lips held hers captive, she felt her love for him swell up in her body.

She moved closer and still closer until she felt that she was a part of him.

He kissed her at first very gently and then more demandingly.

The wonder and glory of it swept over them both.

They felt that the sunshine was moving within them and carrying them up into the sky.

Alister raised his head.

"I love you," he murmured, and his voice was very deep. "I love you as I have never loved anyone else. I could not go on living here or anywhere else without you."

"I love you too," Georgina whispered. "I love you and I did not know that love could be so wonderful."

"You are the softest, the sweetest and the gentlest woman I could ever imagine. You gave me your mind, your body and your soul when I was unconscious and I knew then that you were the only woman for me in the whole world."

There was no need for any more words.

Alister kissed her again and she felt as if he carried her up into Heaven.

She knew that they were in a Heaven of their own.

They were together and their hearts were beating as one.

They were in The Castle which was to both of them a Heaven on earth.

"I love you, I adore you," Georgina whispered to him again.

"And I love you, my darling, my precious," Alister sighed. "You have given me the happiness I thought I would never find. When I am well, we will be married here at The Castle and we will rule our Kingdom together."

Then he was kissing her again.

She knew that her prayers had been answered and God had given them both the love which comes from Heaven, the love which, because it came from Him, would make their life a Heaven on Earth.